Three Christmas Tales

Three Christmas Tales

by

Crystal Linn

Linda Buroker

Setsuko (Sue) Barlow

Martin's Muses

Edmonds, WA

Notice:

1-The characters in <u>Home for Christmas</u> and <u>A Christmas Baby</u> are
all fictional and any resemblance to a real person or persons, living
or deceased, is entirely coincidental.

2-The Amish dialect in <u>Home for Christmas</u> is slightly different
than the dialect in <u>A Christmas Baby</u>. This was intentional as the
stories take place in two different locations, where dialect is different.

Cover photo by Brian Linn of Exploring Imagery, used with permission.

Cover design by Setsuko (Sue) Barlow, used with permission.

Dedications

Crystal Linn

To my brother and sister-in-law, Rex and Cindy Martin,

who have always been there for me

Linda Buroker

To the Edmonds Senior Center

for encouraging lifelong learning

and

To Crystal Linn (Facilitator: on-going writers group)

for making us believe all things are possible

Setsuko Barlow

To dog lovers everywhere,

without my dog my stories would not have been born

Contents

Acknowledgements

I wish to thank the following people for making this book possible:

Linda Buroker for her willingness to publish her new novella in this collection;

Setsuko (Sue) Barlow for her cover design, and her willingness to publish more Yusami stories in this collection;

Brian Linn of Exploring Imagery for his cover photo;

Shirley Feurer for her editorial input.

Crystal Linn
Edmonds, WA
2015

Yasumi's Christmas Adventures

Setsuko Barlow

Introduction

Hi, my name is Yasumi and I am a ten-year-old basset hound. I was given a Japanese girl's name which means 'peacefully beautiful' and refers to my easy-going disposition.

Since my human mom published stories about me entitled, Yasumi's Tail, my name has appeared on the internet a lot. It is amazing to see how many Yasumis are out there, not only as a girl's name but it also used as 'haru-yasumi' (spring break), 'natsu-yasumi' (summer break) and more. Believe it or not, there are tens of thousands of Yasumis listed online.

Although my mom wrote stories about my adventures with her family, there are still more stories to be told. Yasumi's Christmas Adventures contain just some of them.

I think that Christmas is the most globally celebrated festivity, next to New Year celebrations. Even in my mom's birthplace, Japan, the people celebrate Christmas by eating a special cake on Christmas day. No matter where you live geographically, people celebrate Christmas according to their own cultural context. Since my mom immigrated to the USA long ago she values American traditions. We do celebrate Christmas like anyone else living in this country. Christmas is an annual event and a busy season for everyone. We honor the day with joy and happiness at gatherings with family members. We also exchange presents and the children have a lot of fun.

This is my favorite time of the year. When Christmas approaches my family will get busier and anything can happen from time to time. I must step in to help them.

Please join me as I share my adventures with my family during Christmas times, and I do hope you will enjoy reading my tales in Yasumi's Christmas Adventures.

–Yasumi

Happiness is Sleeping

Bang! The loud sound of a car door shutting woke me up.

Mom was finally home. I was so excited to see my mom since she left home ages ago. Actually, I was bored with being left home alone. In this kind of situation, there is nothing I can do except sleep. If I use my imagination, perhaps I could have done a lot of things and even had fun. But then, if I have too much fun chances are I would get into some sort of trouble. It is not worth trying for so I just go to sleep. It's better to save my energy for something important later. It does not matter when and where I sleep, but I usually will get a good nap. In that sense, I served my reputation as 'Miss No Motion' very well.

It is strange for anyone to think that the sound of shutting a car door is actually wonderful. Some people may see it as annoying. But when I heard that sound, I could feel my tension released immediately and I gained a feeling of relaxed peacefulness and happiness. It was like the dynamic ending of Beethoven's Symphony No.9 when all came to an end. I love the great ending when all of the instruments come together to make a strong finish, and it is a wonderful feeling of satisfaction.

As soon as I heard the car door, I jumped off my bed in the hallway upstairs and ran toward the front door to greet my mom. I was so excited to see her. I wagged my tail in a circular motion and then moved from right to left and from left to right constantly—I was unable to control myself. I felt like I was dancing in the air as my whole body shook and bounced.

"Click, click, click..." When I took seven steps down to get to the front door hurriedly, I saw the doorknob turning. Just then, the door was opened and quickly shut.

Bang! My mom and I collided and fell down on the entrance floor. I was stunned for a moment and did not remember what happened. Mom slowly got up and said, "Get out of my way!" She struggled to her feet to run upstairs as fast as possible, rushing through the hallway into the bathroom.

A few minutes later, she came out from the room and said, "I feel so much better now," with a smile on her face.

"Huh?" I did not understand what just happened.

"Bye, see you later," said Mom and then she was gone with the wind.

What was that? I was perplexed. I felt like a whirlpool had swept by. I thought that she was going to stay home as it was late afternoon, and Dad would be home shortly.

Recently, Mom had gone out a lot. So I could not spend much time with her anymore. It got even worse as Christmas approached. I thought that the holiday would bring happiness for everyone. How can a busy person like Mom be happy if she is always busy as a bee building its hive? I wonder how a busy person can have such happiness. As far as I see, my mom is always doing something, so when does she have time to enjoy herself? Perhaps, she feels happy when she is busy? Some people said that happiness just won't come by itself, and one must let it happen. I know who can bring happiness to the family. I believe that Mom will get a lot of happiness soon, because she works so hard all the time.

What is 'happiness' anyway? I wonder if it is the same feeling we have sometimes about ourselves? I feel good when I get lots of sleep after eating a soup bone or meat. I wonder if my happiness is sleep.

Christmas Tree

"Get away!" Dad scolded me as he walked upstairs carrying the tree in an upright position. This was after Mom moved the roll-top desk and cleared the area in the living room. The six-foot-tall fully-branched tree was not easy to move up the stairway. The tree bounced off the walls on the left and right a few times as Dad carried it up the stairs.

"Watch out!" Dad yelled. "I almost dropped it."

"It was not my fault," I told myself.

"Yasumi, get out of the way," he said.

My dad has an attitude, I thought to myself.

"Watch out!" he yelled.

I am here to help him, but...

He quickly moved to the right side and held onto the tree that was tilting. He did not let anyone get near him. Through the opening in the kitchen to the dining area, then to the living room, Dad finally made it. The hardest part was over.

As night drew on, we finally finished decorating the tree. Dad placed the Christmas lights around the tree that were chained to the electrical wire while emitting red and green colors that sparkled. Okay, okay, people said that dogs cannot see colors. However, we can see things that are different from ordinary lights. For example, sparkling lights are quite different from the ordinary lights. These lights appeared and disappeared in a couple second intervals. It would be wonderful to be able to see in colors, but we do not miss it. We don't even know what colors are. We managed to live our life without seeing colors.

Dad played Silent Night on the CD player and it created the mood for Christmas.

"Is everyone ready?" Dad asked.

"Yes!" everyone said in unison.

"There it is."

"Wow!" I barked impressed by the lights that just flashed in front of my eyes.

"Awesome." Bob said.

"Cool." his older brother, Rich said.

"Beautiful." Mom said.

"Good." Dad said.

Our tree was lit and ready for Christmas. We all enjoyed gazing at the tree that was decorated at last, and we felt a sense of pride and satisfaction. Soon, everyone proceeded with his and her own priorities. Dad went downstairs to watch a show on TV, Mom started cooking dinner, and Bob and Rich went to their rooms to play on their computers. But I stayed in the living room and watched the flashing lights a little longer. Although I saw everything in black and white, like in an old photograph, the ornaments reflected in the lights and the shapes came in all sizes and looked spectacular. They came on and off constantly and looked like the lights were chasing each other. It looked like an unknown fantasy world I've never imagined before. It was fantastic.

There were many balls in different sizes hanging from the tree. Because the area was sparkling, I walked toward the tree. I pushed a ball with my nose lightly. It swung while reflecting glittering lights and looked even prettier.

"It's pretty," I thought to myself. So I did the same to another ball as well. It was pretty as well, and it was fun to watch the ball appearing and disappearing while swinging.

Let's try another one, my inner thoughts suggested.

As soon as I pushed the ball with my nose, it came off the tree. "Ding!" It dropped to the floor. "Whoops," I must have touched it a little harder that time. *Gently, gently…* I told myself.

Just then, when I was trying to reach out to the other balls, a silvery garland came off and hung down from the tree. "Whoops."

I wondered what that was and thought I'd better check it out. I quickly investigated while sniffing but it had no smell. And it was not edible. So I checked the balls as well. Nope! I could not eat them either. They were pretty to look at but could not be eaten. Even if they were edible, I probably would not like the taste anyway.

I must retire to my bed before my mom finds out what happened. She probably would not even notice anything that was different though.

Yasumi Claus

"Yasumi, come here," Mom called.

For few seconds, I thought that I was hearing it in my dream. "Yasumi!"

I opened my eyes halfway and looked around, but Mom was not seen anywhere. I then heard it again.

"Yasumi!"

It was coming from the living room.

Do I have to get up now? I still felt sleepy and would like to sleep some more. *But if I do not listen to her she won't be happy. Oh well, I must sacrifice myself for her and find out what's she is up to,* I argued with my inner voice.

"Click…click…click…" I took steps slowly toward the living room.

"Yasumi, come here," Mom said and had a big smile on her face when she saw me.

Huh? What is she up to? I wondered.

"You are going to be a Santa." Mom said excitedly.

Me? Santa? I looked quizzically at her. How ridiculous it sounds. She must be kidding. How can that be possible? I am not even a human and am only a basset hound.

"Try this on," Mom said while she put the outfit on me.

I have never seen it before and did not know what it was. So I just let my mom do all the work while I stood by her.

"This is so nice," Mom was happy to see me in it while her hands busily moved all over me.

First, she put my right front paw through its opening and then my left front paw. She then covered my back with it before she used a belt to secure it.

"Have you gained weight a little?" Mom asked when she tied the belt.

"I do not think so, how about you?" but Mom did not understand my grumblings. While she dressed me up, she pulled forward and backward, smoothing it out. After she fixed the outfit on me she put a Santa hat on my head.

"How cute," she exclaimed.

Why is she so excited? I am only doing this for her.

"Now, you really look like Santa Claus...Yasumi Claus."

You've got to be kidding! I thought. I did not feel comfortable wearing that stuff, so I shook my head. The hat came off.

"Yasumi, you have to wear it!" Mom raised her voice.

I may look like a basset Santa to my mom, but my whole body felt tight and squashed and uncomfortable. I could not even move freely. My chest was tight and I felt like choking. I also felt like I was invaded by a foreign object on my head, so I shook my head. The hat came off. But my mom put it back on my head again. I did not quit and shook my head more. It came off again. It became a competition between my mom and me to see who has more physical endurance. Not only physical strength, but it was also matter of principle. Who is going to believe me as Yasumi Claus? My mom does not think as I do. I thought that she lost her sensitivity. She was weird. Soon, my mom stopped putting the hat on my head, and asked Bob to bring his camera lights to the living room. Good, Mom finally quit doing that. I felt victorious over her.

"Mom, where shall I place these?" Bob asked.

"Place one in the corner here and the other one in the opposite side," she instructed him.

When Bob was placing the lights, Dad came to see what was going on. Mom had also brought her camera with her and set it on the tripod.

As soon as Mom moved the coffee table and some of the chairs, to clear the area, Bob placed the second light as Mom instructed. Our living room was transformed into a photo studio. And, we do have a beautiful model named Yasumi.

The idea of taking Christmas photos of me at home was my dad's idea, and Bob and Mom chipped in their time to help on the family project. Dad became a director. Bob became Mom's assistant and Mom was the camera person.

"Have Yasumi sit by the tree," Dad suggested.

"Yes, it is a good idea. It's good to have Yasumi in front of the tree," Mom agreed.

"Bob, help Yasumi to get ready. Put the hat on her," Mom said and moved the tripod in the spot so that she could capture a good image of me on her camera.

"Is everyone ready?" Dad asked. Bob turned on the lights. "Take Number One," Dad directed.

As soon as the lights were turned on, Mom clicked the shutter on the camera. It was so bright that it blinded my eyes, and I could not see anything around me. I felt nervous, so I tried to run away from the spot.

"Bob, move Yasumi a little closer to the tree," Mom said.

"Okay."

"Yasumi, move to the tree a little," Bob said.

"Okay, that spot is perfect," Mom said and snapped the shutter on the camera.

As soon as Bob moved his hands away from holding me, I shook my head and the hat came off.

"Put it back on her head!" Mom said.

"Okay."

"Good girl! Stay there, Yasumi!" Bob said and tried to calm me down while holding me.

"Hi, Yasumi, look at me," Mom said, trying to get my attention. "Here, Yasumi!" Mom said.

I moved again and again, so Mom missed taking pictures of me.

"She won't stay in the same position any more than a couple of seconds!" said Mom, frustrated.

I am a real dog and not a model or a robot.

Dad had an idea and brought a dog cookie. "Here is a cookie. Do you want to have a cookie, Yasumi?" Dad asked.

"Sure!"

As soon as Dad gave me the cookie, I started to chew it while ignoring Mom.

"Yasumi, look up." Mom said.

Instead of looking at Mom, I shook my whole body and then walked away.

"Stop her!" Mom yelled.

When Dad and Bob were trying to stop me, one of them ran into one of the lights.

"Bang!" the light fell onto the floor. The noise scared me even more and I ran faster. Dad and Bob were racing to catch me.

"Yasumi, wait!" Dad yelled.

"Yasumi!" Bob called.

Dad came from one side and Bob came from the other side in the hallway and trapped me. I had no place to go. I was caught and brought back to the living room studio for more photos to be taken.

"Again?" I sighed.

"Okay, is everyone ready?" Dad asked.

"Yes."

"All right: Take Number Two."

Mom snapped the shutter quickly multiple times as soon as Bob released me. "Yasumi, good girl, look at me." Mom said.

I looked at her for a second, but I turned my head and lay down on the floor.

"Okay, that's good, too." Mom said while snapping the shutter.

"I hope I've captured some good images of her," Mom said. Mom expressed her frustration that I would not cooperate for the pictures. It would be hard for anyone to take pictures of me, because I hate having pictures taken.

So you see, it was impossible for me to become the Santa because I am only a basset hound and not a human. I knew it from the beginning, but why did my family not believe me? I really hope that Mom had some good photos because I do not wish to do that again. I hope that she can find good photos so that she can send them to her relatives.

I only had one cookie through the whole process that day. Now, I understand that the meaning of 'no work and no gain'. But why should I care?

Cookie Taster

Because my mom forgot to buy four boxes of butter beforehand, she had to go to the store again to get them. When she came home a little after 8:00 p.m., she fixed a quick and simple dinner to feed the family. Then she did the dishes and put them away to clear the kitchen, so she could work freely. She got everything ready. This was the time I waited all day for. This was a once-a-year event for my mom, and she spent the evening making cookies. Everyone, especially me, was counting on her. Sometimes things got too crazy in the kitchen, like in a mad house. I remember the time when I ate six pies, which Mom described in her book <u>Yasumi's Tail.</u> Oh yes, those pies were really yummy. As a result, I was punished the next morning. Since I have experienced eating human food, I prefer it. I love its tastes and love to taste all kinds of human foods, such as meat, fish and sweets – anything that humans eat. I hoped I would get to taste her cookies. If I behaved myself accordingly, I am sure that my mom would let me have some cookies.

She usually made all kinds of Christmas cookies from simple sugar cookies to the fancy fruitcakes; whatever her mood was set for. I really did not know what she would actually make, so my guess was as good as anyone's. She had to have energy to do so. Most importantly, she must have all of the ingredients and cooking tools.

I love to be a taster. I would not wait a second to volunteer to be the tester to taste Mom's cookies. I know I am a great one because I have such a superb nose amongst dogs (except bloodhounds)—that's why some people use us for hunting rabbits. Even when a dog is walking across the street from my home I can still smell it. I'll bark at them to let them know that I am here and watching. I do not need to see the dog to smell it, because I know the smell of dogs. I am proud to have such a keen nose and use it effectively. Not only can I smell dogs and the other animals, but I also can smell all kinds of food. My specialty is human's food.

Mom does not know how lucky she is to have me around. For example, I can clean the floor as fast as she drops a piece of meat or cookie dough. She does not need to have a vacuum cleaner. All she needs is me. I do the job with no cost to her. It is a win-win situation.

Mom placed everything she needed on the kitchen counter and was ready to start. "There you go, Mom!" I cheered her on.

"Now listen, stay away from me," Mom warned me.

"Of course, I'll sit away from you and just watch," I assured her with a happy sigh.

"Don't forget," Mom said.

Mom turned the pages of her old cookbook that had been terribly worn over the years. I do not know what that means, but she seemed attached to the book.

Many people do not know about Mom's cooking or baking. Her secret is that she takes the original recipe and modifies and makes completely different food at the end. Sometimes, it will come out really good, but on some occasions, it turns out to be a disaster. For example, she sometimes uses margarine instead of butter, she might use honey instead of sugar, or perhaps skim milk instead of cream and so on. She usually adds or takes out something from the original recipe.

I was curious to see what kind of cookies would turn out.

She put one cup of butter that was previously softening into the mixing bowl and turned on the mixer. As soon as she set its speed in the middle, the mixer moved faster while spitting and throwing the butter everywhere. As a result, the butter splashed on the countertop and on the floor.

"Oh no!" Mom yelled.

"What happened, Mom?"

"Move away!"

It is time for me to step in and help my mom. I thought, *No problem, I can clean it in no time.* I was happy to help my mom cleaning the floor. I licked the butter that had splashed on the floor while Mom was wiping the countertop with a hand towel. I enjoyed the new taste.

"Yum, the butter is creamy and smooth. I like it," I thought to myself.

I moved from one spot to another while licking and helping my mom clean off the buttery spots from the floor. I did not mind this kind of help at all. Mom does not know, but I really enjoyed doing it. That was a wonderful opportunity for me and doesn't happen very often. I took full advantage of it. It is strange to think that I actually enjoyed Mom's mistake. Does that mean the more she makes mistakes, the more I enjoy?

In that sense, I wish Mom makes a lot of mistakes. Am I a bad girl to wish for her mistakes?

Mom started all over again. She mixed all ingredients very carefully, especially handling the mixer. I did not mind staying by her and helping. But if I got in her way, I was chased away. She warned me already. So I graciously moved a few steps away from her and watched.

She used a spoon to drop the cookie dough onto the baking sheet. She filled it with one dozen of those spooned mounds. She placed the sheet into the preheated oven at 350 degrees for fifteen minutes.

"We have to wait for fifteen minutes," Mom told me.

I can hardly wait. Soon, the smell of sweetness came from the oven and became stronger as it rose into the air in the kitchen. The smell drove me crazy. I drooled while inhaling the sweetness. Those were probably the sugar cookies.

"Don't ruin the cookies, Mom," I told her.

"I won't," she said reading my anxiety through my whimpers, whining and groans.

"Don't over-bake Mom," I said.

"I set the timer for fifteen minutes, so it should be all right," Mom said to herself while double checking the recipe.

"But, you over-bake cookies sometimes," I said,

"Because they were under-baked," Mom explained, again reading my concerns.

Mom explained why her baking sometimes turned out over-baked. They were under-baked when she checked them for the first time. She then reset the timer and baked them a little longer, those happened to be over-baked. Mom also read about the temperature setting on the oven. Even though the temperature was set at the same degrees throughout the whole process, the degree of heat was different. For example, in the beginning, the temperature starts up slowly and rises to the point set. But if the heat was there already, the temperature would quickly rise to the higher degree faster. So it is better to preheat the oven for 10-15 minutes before baking, or reduce the setting by a few degrees, or reduce the amount of time by a few seconds on the second or third baking.

While Mom was waiting for the cookies to be baked, she prepared a few more baking sheets full of those spooned mounds so they were ready to go into the oven. As Mom and I heard the sound of the timer ticking, our tension rose, like Mom once saw in a James Bond movie. In the movie James Bond had only eighteen seconds to find the switch and turn off the ticking bomb. I could imagine how the movie viewers felt by watching that particular scene in the movie, tension, tension and more tension. Everyone froze up. However, in this case, the sound of the timer's ticking was actually one of happiness. That means that the cookies were now baking and each second was getting closer to being done.

"Ding!"

We heard the timer hit the finishing point and stop.

"That's it." Mom said happily.

"Yes!" I was so happy to hear that.

Mom opened the door and checked the cookies. "Not quite ready yet," she said and closed the door.

"Huh?" I was disappointed.

"A few more minutes," Mom said.

"A few more minutes?" I whined.

"You heard me," Mom said.

A few minutes seemed far away, but finally the time came. Mom opened the door and checked the cookies again.

"Oh!' she said. "Over-baked," she sighed.

"Oh no," I said.

Mom quickly took the towel that was hanging by the oven and opened the door. As she was taking out the baking pan, she exclaimed, "Ouch!" She then dropped it. The next sound I heard was, "bang" the baking pan fell onto the floor. I rushed to see it.

"Get away," Mom yelled.

Dad heard the noise and came quickly to see what was going on. "What happened?" he asked.

"I burned my finger," Mom said and moved quickly to the kitchen sink and turned on the water.

She put her finger under the running water for a while.

"Do you want to ice it?" Dad asked.

"Yes, it is better to ice my finger," she said.

"Are you in pain?" Dad was concerned.

"A little but I'll be all right," Mom replied.

"You should have used the oven mitten," Dad said.

"I know, but I was in a hurry," Mom answered.

When Mom and Dad were taking care of Mom's burned finger, I checked the cookies. Indeed, the cookies were hot and could not be eaten right away. Somehow I was able to manage and ate some of them though. Mom would not want the cookies that were on the floor anyway. She did not care that I was eating, because she did not say anything about it. She did not even pay attention to me. In the meantime, I helped Mom clean the floor as much as I could. Dad brought a broom and took care of rest of the mess.

"Do you want butter on your finger?" Dad still asked.

"No, I'm okay," said Mom.

"Do you need any other help?" Dad asked.

"I'll be okay, really and thank you," Mom said.

So there, that was how Mom's baking event started. Of course, I had tasted Mom's first sugar cookies. They were as good as usual. I am glad that Mom did not change the recipe. After Dad knew that Mom was all right, he went back to his room. Although Mom burned her thumb, she was able to use it and made all kinds of cookies that night. She also made a pan full of chocolate brownies, a chiffon cake, and we must not forget her favorite, chocolate chip cookies. I wanted my mom to know that I was always here to help whenever she needed. I saw a small spot on her finger, but I was glad that her finger was not burnt terribly. I was also glad that I could help my mom cleaning the floor. I thought she would appreciate it.

Searching for Water

"Help!" I howled.

I had not seen any people, dogs or birds for a long time, not since I was separated from my family. Where was I?

I walked hours under the scorching sun searching for water. My mouth was dry and I wanted to drink some water. Not only I had not drunk water, but I also had not eaten food for a long time. I could not even howl anymore. I was too exhausted to walk forward, and even my four paws would not support me. So I crawled on the sand.

Oh, I feel as if I am baked by the sun! I murmured.

I felt some breezes. But they were warm, like I was taking a sauna bath, and they did not help my comfort level at all. Where was I?

I had never seen any place like this before, no humans, no animals, no birds, no mountains, and no river – nothing, except the sand. The sand dune stretched for miles and miles in the distance and I could not see the end. I had no idea how long that would continue. And I heard nothing; total silence. I missed the people that usually walked by our home. I missed the dogs that barked at me while walking by our house. I missed the squirrels that came to our yard in the morning. I missed the crow that scolded me while it sat on the tree. Most of all, I missed my family.

Where is everyone? Am I in the different world? And...why? I did not understand it.

"Help!" I cried out. No one heard me. Wait a minute. Something was there. I was so happy to see an object that I crawled as much as possible on the sand. In a few moments it was gone. *Where did it go? I just saw it.*

I could not understand anything anymore. Was I beginning to see things? Was I crazy? It did not make any sense. My mouth was dry. I could not even open my mouth to howl anymore, because sand got into my mouth and I had a feeling of choking as I tried to howl for help."

"H...e...l...p!"

"Yasumi?"

All of sudden, I heard Mom calling me. I was so glad to hear that. Oh, Mom was here. After tossing, turning and struggling for a while, I opened my eyes. Where was I?

I looked around and found out that I was on my bed.

I was home. "Hooray!" I howled in my happiest dog voice.

I was so happy to find out that I was not in the desert. I had a nightmare. How terrible it was. I shook my body and got off my bed and slowly walked toward the kitchen. I felt tired but craved for water even more. The house was so quiet, and I heard nothing.

"Where is everybody?" I wondered. As I was walking toward kitchen, I bumped into the wall in the hallway. Whoops. Although I felt sluggish and had lost all of my energy, I dragged my paws in the hallway. My thirst did not go away. I still felt residue from the scorching heat that came from the sun in the desert. I made it to the kitchen with a great effort at last. But there was no water. I just could not believe it. My water dish was empty. Is it possible?

Empty? What happened to it? I always had water in the dish at any time and any day. I did not understand it. No water? So I went to downstairs to look for water. Not only I found no water there, but I also found that the door to the bathroom was closed. I could not even get into the bathroom downstairs. It was my last hope. It was very strange. I would not even try to find water in boys' bedrooms, because they would not keep water there. I then took steps slowly, click…click…click…I went upstairs and searched for water again. Water must be somewhere in the house. It must be.

I looked diligently everywhere. Oh yes! I had learned from my dream and had an idea. When I was lost in the desert, in my dream, I looked for vegetation. Water must be in the ground, the place where vegetation grows. If I dig deeper, I might find water. Even if I find no water, there would be roots of that vegetation. And I could chew the root. I did not give up yet and searched for water. But there is no such luck. I had not seen anything that was green in the room except for our Christmas tree that was standing firmly— and a few of Mom's plants. Since the Christmas tree was cut and brought to our living room as a decoration, it had no roots. It would unlikely grow in the ground again. And mom's plants do not look like there might be water in the dirt either. Besides, Mom would not be happy if I dug the dirt in the pots. Just in case...

Something was calling me to check the tree. I had no idea what that was. But I approached the tree as if I was magnetized by it. As I got close to it, I smelled the pine tree. My mom placed a red colored skirt on the base of the tree and I could not even see the roots.

Do not give up yet, my inner voice said. As I was encouraged, I searched carefully. I slowly put my nose under the skirt and pulled it. I felt coldness on the tip of my nose. What do you know? Beneath the firmly standing tree, I found a stand at the bottom, which helped the tree to a straight, upright position. The stand was also made into a reservoir, so that the tree could have water all the time.

What a clever idea, I told myself. *Indeed, it had water in it – water!"* I whimpered with joy. I was so happy to find water at last. I felt like I found an oasis in the desert. I gulped water from it until I quenched my thirst. I then slowed down and drank more. It was so delicious. I hadn't had water so tasty for such a long time.

After that day, I often drank water from our Christmas tree's reservoir. I did not think that the tree would drink water, because I had never seen it drink water. But strangely though, when I went to have water the next time, there was less water in it. Later, it had even less water in it. I do not think anyone else would drink water from it. Only the tree and I knew about water there. Mom would not know about my drinking it yet, because she did not say any-thing about it. Three days later, Mom poured some water in it be-cause it had dried completely.

I hope my mom did not suspect my drinking that water. I would like to save it for an emergency. Well, she still had not said anything about it.

Night Investigator

As days passed, more Christmas presents arrived and were placed under our Christmas tree in the living room. Some presents arrived from Japan by mail. Inside the packages, Japanese delicacies, in elegant little boxes, were individually wrapped with fancy papers that had traditional Japanese patterns. Mom always appreciates such Japanese delicacies and said, "They make them so pretty!" She also received presents from her friends, and Rich and Bob's friends also dropped off some presents. Mom went shopping frequently. She then wrapped presents and placed them under the tree. It was fun to watch presents piling up under the tree, and the pile seemed to grow all the time. Some were for Grandpa and Grandma and those presents would stay under the tree until Christmas morning. We still had a few days left to shop, so I was expecting to see more presents arrive. Each present had to compete to secure its space under the tree, because it became too crowded after a while.

As my mom got more active during the holiday season with shopping, cooking and visiting friends, my taste buds also became more active. It was because of the goodies Mom made since she was cooking at home more. From the smells of baked potatoes to the pleasant aroma of roast beef in the oven, along with steamed fresh broccoli and brown gravy, everything smelled so delicious and mouthwatering. I could hardly wait for dinner. As I already mentioned earlier, I have a keen nose and my breed has the second strongest nose in the dog world, so I can smell very well and even find other odors. Having such a strong nose does not mean that it is good. Most of the time, I feel frustrated because I cannot eat things I smell. I'm sure that I can smell better than people can. Was I only able to inhale the smell but not able to eat? That was a torture for me. Whether or not I can see the food, I can smell it. Sometime, I would get to eat. Until then, I had to wait patiently while drooling and inhaling the smell.

Patience, patience and more patience, I sighed. *How long do I have to wait?*

"Patience is virtue," Mom had said.

"Really? How so?"

I thought I would ask Mom later to explain it for me. Sniffing and snooping around the presents under the tree became my daily activity. It was fun to check the packages under the Christmas tree. The more presents that arrived, the more I had to investigate. I did not mind that at all, and I enjoyed doing it. So I appointed myself as 'Night Investigator' and I worked at night. I would wait until everyone went to bed, and I would start to investigate the wrapped packages under the tree. Slowly and quietly, I walked toward the living room by the tree and nosed around. I checked each box, nosing it to see if it was the same, or if it had different odors from the others. I checked each present, small and large. Most of the time, I found nothing unusual about those presents. But when I investigated the presents one day, they immediately caught my attention.

They were wrapped nicely with a beautiful wrapping paper and smelled very different from the others. I suspected there was something inside I might like. If I could read the writing, I would know who it was from and to whom. My instinct told me to go right ahead and open it. So I sniffed and checked it. But my conscience still held me back and told me *you must not open it!* Mom already told me to be patient.

"Patience is virtue," she said.

I sniffed again. The more I sniffed, the more I wanted to open it. As Mom told me, I waited a little while. She did not say how long I had to wait. It's not that I did not wait, but I thought I waited enough. Mom would understand.

What the heck? I pushed the box with my nose against the wall, and I then tore the wrapper little by little, and I ate what was in it. These were the familiar taste of dog cookies. The small bites were easy to eat, and I ate them quickly. I then moved to the other package next in line. The package was a little bigger than the first one and had an odd shape. As I tore the wrapper as I did before, a dried beef bone appeared. I gnawed it and got off as much of the meat as possible before I stopped. I could not eat it anymore, so I left it there. After eating these goodies, my conscience bothered me.

I wonder if I should have waited a little longer. *On other hand, I did wait a little longer,* I thought. *But Mom did not tell me how long I should wait,* my inner voice spoke. My inner voice told me to go right ahead and open it. *Which one should I take Mom's wisdom or my instinct? Did I do it wrong this time?* I asked my inner self. *I am only copying Rich and Bob, so it's not solely my own idea.* I justified to myself because the following is what I saw the other day:

"Hey Bob, Mom is gone!" said Rich happily.

"Yeah?" Bob said.

"Mom placed a new present under the tree last night!" said Rich excitedly.

"Yeah?" Bob smiled.

"Come here and see it yourself," Rich said.

So Rich and Bob walked faster to the living room where our Christmas tree was standing.

"This one!" Rich said while picking it up.

"Cool!" Bob answered.

"Who is that for?" Bob asked.

"It says, "To Bob," Rich replied.

"Cool!" Bob burst out.

Rich handed it to Bob. And Bob checked it. Yes, it is surely written as, "To Bob" on it. Bob put it high in the air while holding it; he then brought it by his ear and shook for a few times. No noise came from it but it was heavy.

"I wonder what that is," Bob said.

"Let's check inside, Bob," Rich was eager to see what was in there and encouraged his brother.

"No. Mom would get upset," Bob said.

"Mom would not know. She is too busy lately and would not know what's going on," Rich coaxed.

"Do you think that is okay?" Bob asked hesitantly.

"Yeah! Let's open it and see what's there. I have a plan," Rich said.

"Okay," Bob agreed.

As Bob handed the present to Rich, he removed the scotch tape that was placed several places on the wrapper.

"Whoops!" Rich yelled.

"Oh no, see what you did!" Bob cried loudly.

"Don't worry, I can fix it. The scotch tape is too sticky and it won't easily come off," Rich explained.

"But I can see the label from the spot where it was torn a little," Rich said. "Wow!" he shouted.

"What is it?" Bob yelled impatiently.

"It's a Nintendo game machine," Rich shouted.

"Cool!" Bob was so excited to find out what was there.

"Let's open the whole thing," Rich said.

"But..." Bob said hesitantly.

"We cannot put back the wrapping paper anymore, because it's torn terribly. But don't worry, I have an idea," Rich said.

So they removed the wrapping paper and enjoyed seeing what the present was. They handed it back and forth to each other a few times and admired the box.

"It is so cool, Bob," Rich said again and again.

"We have to re-wrap it again, so that Mom won't know about it," Rich explained.

"Okay," Bob said.

"Alright, Bob, you bring scissors and scotch tape from the pantry in the kitchen. I'll bring wrapping paper from the closet downstairs," said Rich.

"Okay," Bob said.

As Bob brought a scotch tape and scissors, Rich also brought the wrapping paper. Rich wrapped the Nintendo game machine with fresh paper and even copied Mom's writing and wrote, "To Bob" on it. He did not put a ribbon or a fancy bow because Mom would not even notice any differences from the original wrapping.

They heard a car parking in the driveway.

"Mom is home," both said together.

"Quick, put the box behind the other presents," Rich said.

"Okay," Bob said.

Mom opened the front door and cheerfully entered the house. She was glad to see that everything was under control.

"Hi boys, did you do your homework?" she asked.

"We don't have any homework now. We are on our winter break," Rich answered.

"Oh yes, that's right," said Mom as she briskly entered her bedroom carrying shopping bags.

"That was close," Rich whispered.

"Yeah," Bob replied.

Rich and Bob looked at each other and smiled while nodding their heads a couple of times. They were assuring each that everything went all right. After that experience, both of them did it again. This time, they opened a present for Rich.

But how long it continued is not yet known – as I said earlier, it was not my fault.

Christmas

I love Christmas because it is a time for celebration and a joyful event for everyone. All of our family will be home and we do have a variety of activities going on all day. The most exciting part for me is to open presents in the morning. I can hardly wait for daybreak. I would think that Rich and Bob feel the same. They probably are wishing for something they put on the Wish List for Santa's Helper the night before. My wish is very simple and easy. I wished for something I can eat. A steak would be wonderful! I have to wait and see what Santa's Helper planned for me.

"Merry Christmas!"

"Merry Christmas!" Mom said while walking in the hallway early in the morning.

"M-e-r-r-y C-h-r-i-s-t-m-a-s," said Rich coming out from his room rubbing his eyes.

Soon Bob followed him and said, "Merry Christmas," with an unclear voice.

"Merry Christmas!" Dad said cheerfully and came to the living room.

"Oh boy, CHRISTMAS!" I was so excited. *It finally came!*

I was so happy to see everyone gathered in the living room that morning.

"Is everyone ready?" Mom asked.

"Yeah!" everyone answered.

"Rich and Bob, why don't the two of you hand out the presents?" Mom asked.

"Okay."

So we began. Everyone received several presents. There was a lot of excitement and laughter and exclamations bounced off each other when we opened our presents.

"Oh!"

"Wow!"

"My goodness!"

"Cool!"

"Awesome!"

It was nice to see that everyone was happy. Even Mom was actually smiling and laughing and enjoying herself that morning. I had received a large cow bone that weighed about 10 pounds. It was like a dinosaur bone to me. I could chew it, play with it— anyway I like. It was mine.

After we opened our presents and had breakfast, my family left to visit the grandparents by catching the ferry to Bainbridge

Island. Although I was left alone, I had a lot of things to do. Since I had new toys including a chewy ball, a squeaky ball and the giant bone, I played with those until I felt tired. I then took a nap on the L-shaped couch in our recreation room downstairs. I slept well since we had a lot of events earlier. I had plenty of food to eat and a lot of water to drink in my dish, so I did not have to worry about anything on Christmas.

My family came home from the grandparents' a little after 8:00 p.m. and brought something special for me. A few pieces from the prime rib that everyone had for dinner. What a wonderful surprise it was.

"There, you are!" said Mom and put a piece of meat into my dish.

"Yummy!"

What a wonderful Christmas I had! *Christmas is my favorite holiday!*" I thought and appreciated everyone for the special day.

Epilogue

This concludes <u>Yasumi's Christmas Adventures</u>. There are a lot more stories to be told, and future publication may be possible.

In the end, we are glad that we can live together happily, regardless of our differences. Yasumi bonded with us and had impacted our lives so much that I could not even imagine life without her. Certainly, Yasumi made a great contribution to our family.

Thank you for reading these stories of mine about our beloved Ya-sumi.

—Setsuko (Sue) Barlow

Yasumi's Favorite Cookies

(Sugar Cookie Recipe)

1 cup butter or margarine, softened
1 cup sugar
1 egg
3 tablespoons cream or milk
1 teaspoon vanilla
3 cups un-sifted flour*
1½ teaspoons baking power
½ teaspoon salt

In a mixing bowl, cream butter and sugar
Beat in egg, cream and vanilla
Stir in flour, baking powder and salt until mixed well
Preheat oven to 350 degrees Fahrenheit.

Options:
Roll out dough and cut with cookie cutters
Drop spoonfuls onto cookie sheet
Roll into small balls then press down onto baking sheet.

Place 1 inch apart, on ungreased baking sheets. Bake 10–15 minutes until golden brown.

Tip: After cookies are cool, spread with a favorite frosting (chocolate, vanilla, strawberry, etc.) then sprinkle with colorful Christmas decorations.

*For self-rising flour, omit baking powder and salt.

About Setsuko (Sue) Barlow

Setsuko Barlow studied Japanese literature at the University of Washington. Her lifelong passion for folklore triggered her translation works of European fairytales, Ghana folktales and Okinawan folktales. She is currently teaching a class on Japanese culture and language at the Senior Center in Edmonds, Washington.

Ms. Barlow lives north of Seattle with her husband, their youngest son and her new basset hound, Hanako.

Contact information:

> 425-776-5706
>
> chinsagu@frontier.com

Other books by Ms. Barlow:

> Yasumi's Tail: Stories of everyday life with the Barlow's basset hound, Yasumi, told from the dog's point of view.
>
> Books available on Amazon
>
> Yesterday, Today and Tomorrow, An Anthology: Ms. Barlow was a contributing author to this anthology.
>
> Books available on Amazon
>
> Ashanti Father (Tales of Ghana): Ms. Barlow translated these folk tales from Ghana.
>
> Book currently in publishing process
>
> Good Night Stories (Western Fairy Tales): Ms. Barlow translated these.
>
> Book currently in publishing process

Home for Christmas

Linda Buroker

Abigail Kaufman scurried toward the kitchen table balancing a platter of ham and eggs in one hand and a hot muffin tin in the other. "Hot, hot, hot," she cried as the heat of the pan burned through the thin towel she had grabbed from the counter to use as a hot mat. Sarah leaned back in her chair, trying not to look alarmed, as the pan of muffins flew past her nose and came to rest perilously close to the edge of the table.

Abigail always scurried. Plump and diminutive in stature she felt a need to run just to keep up with her tall sturdy children. Today her feet were doing double time as she rushed around the kitchen. The proprietor of the Cornucopia Café in downtown Moss Lake was stopping by to pick up the four dozen oatmeal raisin cookies cooling on the counter, and with the Christmas season coming, he was asking for more.

Sarah smiled as she recovered from the near mishap. She knew that her *mamm's* cooking was a labor of love, but she also knew that receiving recognition was against everything the Amish believed in. Pride was a sin and good food, after all, was no more than a source of sustenance.

Sarah was used to her energetic *mamm* but even so she was hard-pressed not to laugh as she intercepted the plate of ham and eggs before it too crashed to the table. "Slow down *mamm*. Mercy! What's the rush?"

"Forgive me *mein kin*, my child. I've allowed myself to get flustered and I've taken it out on you." Abigail had the grace to look apologetic as she spun on her heels and hurried to the sink. She breathed a sigh of relief as she plunged her reddened fingertips into the pitcher of cool water sitting next to the pump.

"Did I miss something? Is there a gathering coming up that I don't know about?" Sarah asked. "*Vhy* are you baking at 5 o'clock in the morning?" She peered over the top of her wire-rimmed glasses at the cookies cooling on the counter, more than enough for two families.

Abigail shrugged and tried to look nonchalant as she announced, "I am baking cookies for Joseph King to sell at his café in town. He *vill* be here in a few minutes to pick up *vhatever* I can have ready."

"How did that come about?" Sarah quizzed as she helped herself to one of the apple muffins which had cooled enough to be eased from the pan.

"Mr. King bought all of the cookies that I made for the Christmas fund-raiser. He sold everything that he didn't eat himself, and his customers loved them. He asked me if I *vould* like to bake for him on a regular basis. I said *ja*, yes, and he has been picking up a few dozen rolls and cookies every morning since then." She paused and Sarah had the odd feeling that her *mamm* was asking for her permission.

Abigail continued, "I love doing it Sarah, and he said he *vould* pay for my efforts." She took a deep breath as if willing herself to slow down. "I *vas* hoping I could make a little extra money so that you wouldn't have to work so hard."

"Oh *mamm*," Sarah groaned, "that is so sweet of you, but we are doing okay, aren't *ve*?"

"*Ve* are, but you shouldn't have to work so hard. I feel awful that you have to take care of Hiram, in his craziness, in addition to your regular job at that 'home'

Sarah understood that her mother felt better about her work at the Retirement Center if she thought about it as a 'home'. The idea that it was a place for people who had nowhere else to go bothered her *mamm* and Sarah knew she tried hard not to think about it. Amish families took care of their elderly. The thought that some people had to grow old in an institution was repugnant to her mother.

"You can't keep taking care of old people forever!" Abigail declared, "It's sad enough that you have to *vork* outside the home at all."

Sarah, as tall and slender as her *mamm* was short and plump, stood and gave Abigail a hug and planted a kiss on the top of her head. It was early in the day but damp ringlets had already managed to escape the confines of Abigail's *kapp*. Sarah smiled tenderly as she tucked the soft brown curls, with just a hint of gray, back where they belonged under the edges of her mother's *kapp*. The hair felt lumpy through the thin material and Sarah wondered if Abigail, in her haste, had donned the traditional head cover without bothering to comb her hair. It wouldn't be the first time. Sometimes Sarah wished she had inherited her *mamm's* carefree spirit instead of always feeling obligated to do the right thing. "Take a minute and have breakfast *vith* me," she invited. "If you enjoy baking you should do it, but not because you think *ve vill* be in the poor house if you don't."

Abigail's head bobbed up and down. "I know, but I like to feel useful and *grossmamm*, your grandmother, really doesn't take up much of my time." Abigail's *mamm* had barely turned ninety when she had come to live with them four years earlier. She was mentally sharp and a joy to have around but her body was failing and she needed help getting around.

Sarah nodded, "It was good of Joseph to think about us." She sat back down and Abigail sat down across from her. She studied her sweet daughter's face. "Exactly," she said. "Having something to do gives us a sense of purpose." Abigail kept her tone bland before switching to the topic that was nearest and dearest to her heart. "It pains me that you have had to put your own plans for having a family on hold and that you have put off being baptized into the church because of your *vork*."

"You know I don't mind *mamm*, it's what families do," Sarah sighed. Was her mother right? Had she given up on having a life of her own? She didn't think so, she wasn't even sure marriage was for her. She liked her work at the Retirement Center and was afraid that she would have to give it up if she was baptized into the faith. Perhaps her job was just an excuse to justify her independent spirit; perhaps she was not a true Amish girl at all. She hadn't been in love since she was thirteen years old. What did that say about her? "What makes you bring that up again? Is someone getting married?" Sarah asked.

Abigail buttered one of the cooled apple muffins and shrugged. "Edmund Weisser, the last bachelor in your circle, is marrying Katie Lapp. It could have been you." She looked at her beautiful daughter. The blonde hair was gathered tidily back in a thick braid. Sarah had peach colored skin and the most beautiful brown eyes imaginable, a gift from her *dat*, her father. Abigail felt once again her youngest daughter should have been married years ago.

Sarah pushed her plate away, the subject of marriage making her lose her appetite. "Edmund never *vas* an option, *mamm*. He has asked every eligible woman in the community to marry him. He just *vants* a warm body to take care of those six unruly children of his. Frankly I'd rather stay single. At least at the Retirement Center I get paid for my labors."

Her *mamm* seemed somewhat calmed as she reached over to pat her daughter's hand but couldn't refrain from shaking her head and saying, "Tsk tsk."

Sarah stood and carried her dishes to the sink. "I'll do *vhat* I can for Hiram until other arrangements can be made. He is crankier than most, but he is sick too, both in body and in spirit." She sighed, "Fortunately, he seems to remember me from the days *vhen* we *vere* young and Matt and I played together." Sarah swallowed painfully at the memory. "Hiram was never *vhat* you would call a nice man. If he hadn't been so hard on his *kinner*, children, they *vould* be here to take care of him now."

"It's a sad story." Abigail admitted. "I remember *vhen* Matt ran away. It was hard on his *mamm*. Everything fell apart after he left. Their daughter married and moved away too and no one has heard from her since. The *gut Gott*, good God, only knows what happened to Matt. He *vas* such a good boy."

Sarah took a sip of coffee, reluctant to meet her mother's eyes. She didn't want to admit that she had been an accomplice in helping Matt run away, but the story needed telling. "His *dat* nearly beat him to death. He came here that night and I helped him. I dressed his wounds, found him a change of clothing, and gave him food from our pantry." She paused to process the sadness that threatened to overcome her before she was able to continue, "He asked me not to tell anyone *vhat* had happened." She didn't add that he had written a few times and she had a vague idea where he was living.

Her *mamm* seemed to accept her story and she nodded sadly, "You *vere* always a good girl. I didn't know."

"That *vas* just it! Nobody *vanted* to know *vhat* was going on up there at Hiram's farm. I'll see if I can find out a little more, perhaps Matt's *mamm* had some letters hidden away. We need to find a family member to help with him."

Abigail nodded although it was obvious that she didn't quite understand the family dynamics. Amish families weren't supposed to be like that, they were there for each other.

"Don't look so worried *mamm*. I'll think of something. Marriage isn't for everyone and I enjoy my work. The Retirement Center has offered to pay for some of us to take college classes in exchange for committing to a few years of work. I am thinking about doing it, but we'll talk more about that later. You get back to your baking. Send along a couple of these muffins too. They're really good."

Sarah primed the pump to spill cool water into the dish pan already filled with boiling water. "I'll clean up here. Is there a basket of goodies to take to Hiram?"

Sarah was no longer an ugly duckling, but her *mamm* was right, life had passed her by. As the youngest daughter she had been left to help her parents after her sisters had left to start lives of their own. They had sold most of the acreage after her father died;

keeping only enough for a vegetable garden and a few animals. She hated to admit it but the money from her mother's business venture would be welcome.

With an added spring in her steps, Sarah felt like she sailed to the top of the hill. Just hearing that she wasn't going to have to think of more excuses for saying no to Edmund lightened her heart but, at the same time, what was she going to do about Hiram? His condition was deteriorating, even with her limited expertise she could tell that. She would have to get a message to Matt and pray that he would answer.

Her fingers caressed the post card in her pocket. Just knowing that she had something belonging to her childhood friend comforted her and made her feel less lonely. He didn't say much, almost as if he was afraid to expose his true feelings, but she knew that he was safe and that he still thought about her. He had sounded sad in his last few notes and she wondered if he missed his old life at all.

The last message had arrived a week ago and was written on the back of a picture postcard of the University Hospital Medical Center in Chicago. Apparently he was still in Illinois and not that far away. It was the only clue she had. He filled the limited space with his careful scrawl, purposely not leaving enough room for a return address, but still he wrote every month. Certainly that was a sign that he was reluctant to let go of all that was familiar to him.

At first she had understood why he had been so guarded about his whereabouts, he didn't want anyone to find him, but now she didn't know. It had been fourteen years and he was a man now. There was no reason for him to think she would be here waiting for him, but her heart warmed at the thought. She had tucked each letter carefully into the hand carved box that he had made for her on her eleventh birthday.

The door to the old Amish farmhouse was ajar and her tentative knock unanswered. She pushed the door the rest of the way open and stepped into the cold dark room. Usually Hiram roused himself enough to touch a match to the logs but there was no welcoming warmth today. "Hiram," she whispered softly. "Are you here?"

A gust of cold air followed her into the already chilly kitchen. Dishes were piled high in the sink and the old wood stove was barely warm. Her initial panic subsided as her eyes adjusted to the gloom. The old man was huddled on the couch under a pile of quilts but the quiet rise and fall of his chest assured her that he was still in this world. At work she was accustomed to making quick assessments but it was different here. She had no clear instructions about what to do. Would anyone care if the old man died?

The mound on the couch moved and Hiram croaked. His voice weak and his cough moist but he still managed to sound disagreeable, "Where else *vould* I be. Shut the door. *Vere* you raised in a barn?"

Sarah flinched even though it wasn't her fault the fire had gone out. She was used to the old man's angry words but it didn't make hearing them any easier. At least he didn't tell her to get out. With a sigh she pulled off her brown woolen cloak, gave it a quick shake, and hung it on the peg behind the door.

How in the world had he made such a mess in one day? She cleared a space on what had once been a beautiful hand crafted table and placed the heavy basket of food in the center. A casserole, two fresh loaves of bread, and a tin of cookies would provide enough food for several days. The Amish women of Moss Lake were determined to take care of Hiram, even though their offers had been repeatedly rebuffed.

"Good Morning Hiram," she called again as she rolled up her sleeves and set to work. "I see the fire went out during the night." He only grunted in reply, so thin and gaunt, a mere shadow of the man she remembered from her youth. They had always been private people and they had managed without help after the children were gone, but when his wife passed on he had no one. It wouldn't be long before he would need total care if he were going to survive.

The Bishop had asked Sarah personally if she would check on Hiram. It was not in her nature to refuse a request, but it bothered her, more than she wanted to admit, that she had become the go-to person every time someone needed something. "Let Sarah do it," they whispered, "she doesn't have anything better to do."

As a rule Sarah was good with people and her patients adored her, but Hiram was not so easily charmed. She was sweet and caring, qualities that made her an excellent caregiver but served to isolate her as well. She had turned down offers to join her friends for social functions so often that they had finally stopped asking her to join them.

The old man was ill and she knew it. It broke her heart and filled her with sadness but she put her feelings aside and set about restoring order. Taking a chance at being rebuffed, she fluffed his pillow and pulled the quilt that had slid to the floor over him once again. He didn't say anything but he watched her every move as she stuffed old newspapers into the wood stove and then placed small pieces of wood on top of them. The fire re-lit easily.

Hiram always had been a terrible housekeeper. When he did stumble out of bed he left messes wherever he went. Most days she had just stopped by at the farm on the hill with a cheery smile and a bag of edibles provided by the women down below, but something was different today. There was more disarray than usual.

After spending all morning restoring order to the house on the hill Sarah was exhausted. Hiram snoozed in the now-warm living room and the house was presentable. She was pleased that he had eaten the plate of food and finished the full glass of milk which she had placed beside the couch. At least she didn't have to coax him to eat or feed him like she did some of the old dears at the home where she worked.

It was after 3 o'clock when she finally sat down to have a bite of lunch herself. She often stayed late because it was quieter here than at home. It gave her a chance to study without feeling like she was doing something dishonest and underhanded. She hadn't mentioned to her *mamm* that she was already taking advantage of the tuition reimbursement program at the Retirement Center. She thoroughly enjoyed her Fundamentals of Nursing classes and she was eager to start on her homework, but first she had to write to Matt. She lifted a piece of lined white notebook paper out of her binder, uncapped her pen and started to write.

Sarah and Matt had been inseparable as children and she had mourned his absence for years, never quite feeling that he was gone for good. She had a crush on him when she had been a scrawny twelve year old and he, two years her senior, was already heartbreakingly handsome and so very grown up. She had been flattered that he came to her in his hour of need.

Sarah stared into space as memories assailed her. What could she say to make him come back home? Matt was the youngest boy with three older brothers and he was less than a year older than his baby sister. The older boys had left home years before Matt had reached his maturity. He had tried hard to be a good son but his quiet, thoughtful ways rubbed on his *dat's* nerves. Frequent beatings became the norm.

On that last night Matt had crawled over to the Kaufman's barn on his hands and knees. He knew that he had to get away. Sarah had been alone in the barn feeding the goats when he had staggered through the open door and collapsed at her feet. She held him close until he calmed and then took it on herself to be the grown up. She washed and dressed his wounds and left him to rest while she scavenged clean clothes from her *dat's* closet. She filled her school backpack with a bottle of water, a loaf of bread and cheese to send with him as she watched him walk out of her life.

She had to reach him somehow. She had to tell him that his mother was dead and that his father was failing. She needed help. He owed her that much, didn't he?

She wrote the letter to the fourteen-year-old boy that she remembered. She let her heart and her fears spill onto the single piece of white paper. Tears blurred her eyes as she folded the page into a tidy rectangle and slipped it in an envelope. Careful to make her letters legible she wrote his name on one line, paused for a heartbeat, before hastily adding the words "in care of the University Hospital Medical Center in Chicago, Illinois."

High winds, heavy snowfall and plummeting temperatures brought downtown Chicago to its knees. Snowplow drivers worked tirelessly to clear the city streets. An endless parade of emergency vehicles delivered hapless victims of the storm to Emergency Rooms throughout the city.

The University Hospital Medical Center, well known for its state-of-the-art trauma center, took the brunt of the calls. The wind howled and the generators moaned but business went on, albeit more chaotic than usual. Stretchers lined the hallways but by dawn most of the patients had been treated and were waiting to be discharged or admitted to the hospital. Weary employees, feeling more than a little shell shocked, peeled off protective gloves and rumpled gowns before heading to the locker rooms.

Dr. Matthew Barnhart, the chief resident of the trauma unit, couldn't remember when he had ever been so tired. He scribbled his name on the last of the charts piles in front of him with such force that he nearly tore the paper. "The rest will have to wait Junie, my replacement just walked in the door."

"One more patient," she wheedled, "there's a pretty blonde in exam room C." June Alexander, the handsome African-American woman who had reigned over the University ER, Emergency Room, for thirty years, was ever hopeful but she didn't expect him to bite. The request was half in jest and he knew it. Matt grinned at her as he finished dotting every 'I' and crossing every 'T'. Nurse Alexander was the heart of the ER and she had taught him well. She made it clear on his first day as an intern that paperwork was important if they wanted to stay out of court and get paid for their efforts.

He raised his eyebrows at her and stifled a yawn. "I can't Junie. My shift is over. In fact it was over before this nightmare began."

"I know," she answered, "but you know me, ever hopeful." She perched on the edge of the desk and looked at him until he fidgeted self-consciously.

"What." He stuttered as he absently fingered his scarred ear, a remnant from his old life.

She swatted at his hand, "Stop fidgeting and leave that ear alone." Matt's ear, damaged in that last fight with his father, still bothered him and he would finger it nervously whenever he was deep in thought. To others, the missing lobe and jagged scar extending down the side of his jaw made him look dangerously appealing, like a pirate. "Don't," she whispered softly taking his hand and giving it a squeeze. "Today is the last day of your residency here at the University. I hope you won't be a stranger. I happen to know you could stay on here for a fellowship if you wanted to," she swallowed hard before adding. "You've turned into a fine young man Matthew Barnhart. I'll miss you more than I can say."

He gave her one of his quiet 'ah shucks' looks and shrugged. "I'll miss you too Junie, but flattery will get you nowhere. Tonight was my last hurrah as your trauma boy. I am officially off duty and no longer covered by the hospital's insurance policy. We'd be up a creek without a paddle if that lovely blonde decided to sue us; I'd have to marry her to keep her from tearing us apart."

June snorted and looked down her long nose, "I'd sue you myself if I thought it would lead to a proposal."

"I'm not good enough for you June Alexander, besides I'd rather stay on the good side of Big John Alexander – your husband. I respect him too much to try and take his woman away." His face was sober when he paused to look up at her, "I was thinking about the night we met. I wouldn't be here if it hadn't been for you."

June had been working the night shift when Dr. Max Krueger had brought a trembling fourteen-year-old boy into the University ER. He had found the boy huddled inside a roadside kiosk and had feared for his life. She had helped the old doctor soak off the soiled makeshift bandages and then administered fluids and antibiotics as directed. It had been her responsibility to follow the hospital's protocol to call the police when abused children arrived at their doorstep, but she weakened. Dr. Max explained that the boy was Amish and had run away from an abusive situation. When she learned that it was doubtful that anyone would be looking for him she looked the other way. For the first time in her professional career she had followed her heart instead of adhering to protocol, and had never regretted it.

Dr. Max had taken the boy to his own home, nursed his wounds and kept him safe. The boy had proven to be well mannered and bright. It had been his delight to guide him into manhood and nurture his interest in medicine.

June shook her head as if returning her thoughts to the present. "Are you going to stay here in Chicago?"

"I honestly don't know. I've had some offers but I haven't had enough time to myself to even think about what I want to do next. Shocking I know, but I can't picture myself going very far away. This has been my home for so long that I think of you all as family."

"If I remember right you are from right here in Illinois. Have you thought of checking in with your family of origin?"

"I've made it a point to stay busy so I wouldn't have to think about that, but yes, I suppose I do need to confront my demons at some point."

"I hope you won't do anything that will hurt Max. You two are so good together. He was practically a recluse after his wife died and you gave him a reason to come out of his self-imposed isolation."

"You know me better than that. He saved my life, you both saved my life. If you had called Social Services they would have sent me home or placed me in foster care and who knows what would have happened to me."

She sniffled, "I've always prided myself on my instincts. I would have taken you in myself rather than send you back where you came from. Well, enough of this warm fuzzy stuff. If you won't see that blonde I'll have to get back to work."

Matt glanced up as she made to move away. "I won't make any life altering decisions without checking in with you."

"You do that," she said gruffly turning her back to him, but not before he noticed that her eyes were teary. She gave a half-hearted wave and hurried into the waiting room to greet and triage the patients waiting for attention.

He stacked the charts he had been working on and handed them to the ward clerk, who had been standing there, to file away. When he looked up again he noticed that Tracy Ellison, one of the new interns, was standing in front of him twirling her stereoscope." What's up Doc?" she flirted mildly.

He leaned back in his chair and gave her a thoughtful look, almost sorry that he had made it a policy not to chat up co-workers. "Glad you made it. It's been a nightmare but we are almost caught up. There are a couple of routine cases waiting for you in Exam rooms A and C. Hopefully the street crews are out in full force by now and everyone who got home unscathed will stay there."

"I'll get right to it then," she sighed, looking back over her shoulder as she walked away. She gave him her best come hither smile but his attention was already elsewhere.

"You will miss all this," she called after him.

He smiled his agreement and said under his breath, "More than you know." Instead of prolonging the conversation he saluted jauntily and headed to the locker room to change clothes. He had been taught better than to be seen in public unshaven and wearing dirty scrubs.

Thirty minutes later an almost refreshed Matthew Barnhart made his way into the cafeteria. He had been eating his meals there for so long that the ladies working the tray line didn't even ask what he wanted. Matt watched Rosa Gonzales dish up a big bowl of oatmeal and butter a toasted bagel for him, the same thing he ate every morning.

She looked at his drawn face and smiled as she tucked extra bowls filled with sliced bananas, chopped nuts, raisins, and brown sugar onto his tray. "Don't you ever get tired of oatmeal Doc?"

"*Holá* Rosita." he greeted her with a smile. Matt was shy around his peers, especially sophisticated young women, but he had no trouble coming out of his shell around comfortable mother figures. "You know that a good Amish boy always starts his day with a big bowl of oatmeal. You are looking particularly fine this morning; you must have some good news?"

Rosa beamed at him, "Oh yes, thanks to you. Roberto has a mentor from the Boys and Girls Club now who helps him with his homework. Roberto got a B on his last Algebra exam and Mr. Manos says he has a real gift for math."

"Kids need someone to look up to at that age. Your English is improving too, is that same gentleman helping you?"

"It is just like you to notice. I am studying hard Doctor Matt. Mr. Manos says I will be ready for the citizen exam by spring, and he wants me to study for my GED next."

Somehow the news didn't surprise him. Matt had been drawn to the cheerful woman who always had a book in her pocket. Now that her son was doing well in school she was eager to improve on her own resume. He enjoyed practicing his high school Spanish with her and she her English with him; they were both doing splendidly. "It sounds like Mr. Manos is a good influence on both of you." He replied.

She blushed and lowered her head. Matt was glad that he had introduced Rosa and her son to his basketball buddy at the Boys and Girls Club. Having people who cared about you makes a difference, he could attest to that. Three people had played pivotal roles in his life too, and he vowed he would never disappoint any of them.

Rosa was only one of the many hospital employees who had opened up to the earnest young doctor who remembered their names and took an active interest in their lives. He would miss them all. It had been like having half a dozen mothers who made sure he got enough to eat. He picked up the sturdy plastic tray, added a pitcher of cream and a glass of orange juice, and made his way past the cash register.

Hands waved to him from nearby tables where his co-workers were rehashing every detail of the evening, but he was too tired to make the effort. Instead he made his way to a lone table by the window. The bright morning sunlight hurt his tired eyes but the light and warmth drew him like a moth to flame. He positioned the chair so that his back was against the window and slumped into it. The window seat gave him an unobstructed view of the huge room that served as the hub of the entire medical center.

He missed winters at home. After morning chores he had been able to relax and read without feeling guilty. While idle hands were not encouraged many accepted the long hours of being housebound as a time to rest and regenerate. Matt had embraced the idea but his father hated that about him.

He closed his eyes and remembered the cold blustery days when he would slip over to Sarah's house. The two of them would settle in front of the fireplace to read or play. Her *mamm* would make cookies and offer cups of her delicious hot chocolate. His mouth watered involuntarily at the thought. He hadn't tasted hot chocolate made from scratch in all the years he had been gone.

In the city it was a different story. The numerous heart attacks, falls and roadside accidents doubled when the weather was bad, but even so the quiet aftermath was mesmerizing. Excited children squealed in the courtyard as they pelted each other with snow balls and rolled balls of snow round and round until they grew into full-bodied snowmen and women. Christmas and children were the same everywhere.

Matt was going to be alone this year, the first time in a long time, and he wasn't sure what he was going to do. Normally he volunteered for extra shifts at the hospital so that his friends could be off, but it wasn't an option now that his tenure was over. Max had invited him to join him and his lady friend for a week of skiing in Vermont but he didn't want to be a third wheel and had tactfully declined.

His thoughts were interrupted when Dr. Melrose, the head of the trauma department, burst through the doors of the cafeteria. Melrose was always in a hurry and today was no exception. Even the way the man dressed defied nature. His scrubs were always tucked in, wrinkles were barely tolerated, and blood spatters un-thinkable. He somehow managed to look as imposing in scrubs as he did in his famous, or infamous, Armani suit: a man on a mis-sion.

The man frowned as he scanned the room until his gaze fell on Matt half hidden in the corner of the room. Matt caught his breath, half tempted to duck out of sight. He has ceased being a resident twenty minutes before, but he still felt like a raw recruit in the presence of the great man. Unbidden he wondered what he had done wrong.

"Dr. Barnhart, there you are! I was hoping to catch up with you before you left. I wanted to thank you for covering for me last night. I was delayed in Boston because of the storm and couldn't catch a flight out until this morning."

Matt half stumbled to his feet but didn't have the strength to resist when the older man waved him back into his chair. "Sit! Your shift is over, as well as my jurisdiction over you. You look beat. Are you safe to drive home?"

"I'm fine. Thanks for asking. I'm staying at Max's while he is away and I can walk from here."

"I hear the old goat is finally going to tie the knot, suppose you'll be next?" he said settling into the chair across the table from Matt.

"I haven't had time for any serious relationships, as you well know. I guess I'm still an Amish school boy at heart, or at least not enough of a 'bad boy' to make the grade with city girls." Matt paused to reflect before continuing. "Max frowned on the idea of dating co-workers so he probably would have given me the heave-ho if I had dared to disobey, besides there is someone back home," he said vaguely trying to deflect the conversation off of his plans.

Dr. Melrose threw back his head and laughed. "We are pretty hard on you kids, although it doesn't seem to stop most of these randy young bucks. They seem to spend more time in the closet and break rooms than on the job," he said. "You are a good doctor Matthew. If you are interested in doing a fellowship in trauma medicine I hope you will come back here."

"Thanks, Dr. Melrose, I appreciate your kind words. I love ER so of course I will think about your offer, but I did promise Max I would take my time. His first love is Family Medicine and I know he would like it if I would spend a year with him."

"You should go back home to Moss Lake and see if that sweetheart is still waiting."

Matt stared up at Dr. Melrose with an incredulous expression surprised that the man had picked up on his remark. "It's been a very long time so I hardly think so. The Amish tend to marry young so the likelihood is slim, besides I hardly consider myself Amish anymore."

Dr. Melrose put on his serious face. "You are more Amish than you know. I keep pretty close tabs on my students and I've been friends with Max for more years than you've been alive."

Matt popped the last bite of his bagel into his mouth and chewed it thoroughly before answering. "It's been fourteen years. We were just kids when I left."

"Go back to see her and make peace with your dad. It will make moving forward much easier. Perhaps this will help you to make up your mind." Dr. Melrose fished a battered white envelop from his breast pocket and handed it to Matt. "This letter has been circulating around the hospital for days and finally ended up at my desk. It is postmarked Moss Lake and might be important."

Matt turned the plain white envelop over in his hand and examined the neat script. It was simply addressed to him in care of the hospital. It had been postmarked two weeks earlier and from its rumpled appearance it was a wonder it had found him at all.

"Thank you sir," Matthew picked up his knife and slit the envelop open with a sense of foreboding. His heartbeat ratcheted up a notch when he saw the familiar handwriting. Sarah was the only one who had any idea where he was.

"Dear Matthew," he read. She wrote with that same small precise handwriting that had been her trademark as a child. *"I hope this finds you well."*

"From the girlfriend I presume," Dr. Melrose said gruffly as he got to his feet. "I'll leave you to it then. Oh, if you are still in town on Christmas Eve my wife would love it if you could join us for dinner, but I will explain if 'other matters' need your attention."

"Thanks you sir. Tell her I would be happy to accept her invitation, if I am still in town. Her culinary expertise is well known and I'd be a fool to refuse." Matt stretched his weary muscles before continuing. "As you know, Max and I are quintessential bachelors and cooking has never been our forte. Most of our meals together were eaten right here in this cafeteria. I'm not sure I remember what real food tastes like, but please ask her not to try and fix me up with anyone. I have too much on my mind right now."

"I'll tell her that you have a girlfriend," he nodded at the letter which Matt had unfolded and was absently smoothing with his fingers, "Now I'll excuse myself and let you read your letter. Keep in touch young man."

Matt smiled his gratitude as he turned his attention back to the letter, reading the words carefully. *"I don't know if you are still in Chicago or not but thought I would try. I'm quite desperate. Your dat is very ill and since your mamm died he is more irritable than ever. He refuses help from the community, which everyone is most distressed about, and we are at our wits ends. He seems to remember me from the old days and he allows me to bring groceries and help him out a little. However his condition continues to deteriorate and I don't know who to turn to. I work full time and have my own mamm and grossmamm to care for so my time is somewhat limited. I am begging you to come home to help me figure out what to do with Hiram. Please, in remembrance of our friendship. Sarah."*

He ran his fingers through his hair and took a deep breath. It was time to go home to Moss Lake.

The cold fresh air nearly took Matt's breath away as he strode through the sliding doors of the emergency room and out into the street. He shoved his hands deep into the pockets of his parka, glad that the wind was at his back, and set off at a brisk pace toward the house that had been his home for the last fourteen years. His beleaguered brain tried hard to process the feelings that Sarah's letter evoked. Memories of that day fourteen years ago, when a kindly old gentleman had scooped him up into his arms and staggered into this very same emergency room and had changed everything, or so he thought.

He was no longer a frightened young boy but that didn't make thoughts of returning to Moss Lake any easier. He kept telling himself as he hurried along that he was a man now and that his *dat* could no longer hurt him.

Right now he needed to sleep more than anything else. He would think about what he had to do tomorrow. Max was away for the holiday and the housekeeper wasn't due in until Friday so the house was still except for the quiet hum of the refrigerator. After unlocking the door and entering then locking it again behind him, Matt kicked off his walking boots and padded quietly down the hall to his room. Without bothering to take off his clothes he crawled under the covers and fell into a deep sleep. He had honed the knack of sleeping hard and fast over the years. Medical students learned early on that sleep was a precious commodity and needed to be dealt with as efficiently as everything else.

Obviously his mind had been busy while his body repaired itself. He had slept the clock around and felt refreshed when he finally surfaced from his deep sleep. He knew exactly what he had to do. It took him less than an hour to shower, pack a small bag, and down a quick a breakfast of oatmeal prepared in the microwave. The oatmeal wasn't anything like the cooked variety that his *mamm* had made when he was a boy, but the milk was cold and the brown sugar sweet. Hot cereal in the morning reminded him of who he was and where he came from. Tidy by nature he rinsed his dishes and stacked them in the dishwasher.

It bothered Matt that it had taken so long for Sarah's letter to reach him. His reluctance to share details of his new life had kept him from giving out his address. He had been wrong. It was doubtful that anyone from Moss Lake would have reported his absence, but he had been afraid and it had been years before he stopped looking over his shoulder. He owed Sarah an apology. They had been best friends growing up and without her help he wouldn't have had the courage to leave.

He had written his last note on a picture postcard that he had found on the table in the residents lounge, had it been a subconscious gesture? Did it mean he wanted to be found?

It took a clever girl to pick up the subtle, or not so subtle, clue. Not a girl, he reminded himself, Sarah would be a woman now with a family of her own, but why was she working and taking care of Hiram as well as her own *mamm* and *grossmamm*? Was she okay? She had been there for him when he needed help and now it was his turn to help her.

He called Max to tell him that he was going to Moss Lake for the holidays and sent a text to Dr. Melrose declining his dinner invitation. Less than an hour later, dressed in warm flannel-lined jeans and a sheepskin jacket, he guided his Jeep Cherokee out of the city and into the heart of Illinois farmland.

The journey that had seemed so long fourteen years ago took less than an hour and a half to drive. The gently rolling farm lands no longer looked familiar and banks of snow obliterated anything that might have triggered a memory, good or bad.

Matt almost missed the turn off for Tipton. Snowplows had worked throughout the night. The roads were scraped clean and sanded but the banks of snow piled high and all but hid the road signs from view. Five miles beyond Tipton a road branched off to the left and became little more than a country lane. Few travelers knew that the Tipton exit was the gateway to remote Amish communities.

The lane hadn't been cleared but it hardly mattered. Motorized vehicles were the exception rather than the rule here in the heart of Amish land. Matt shifted into 4-wheel drive and inched slowly forward, not stopping until he reached the outskirts of Moss Lake.

He blinked, closed his eyes and blinked again. Everything looked different. How could this be? The Amish never changed. The Moss Lake he remembered had been a rural farming depot with only a general store, a blacksmith shop and a post office. Now it looked like a real town. Shops and businesses lined both sides of Main Street and only hitching posts instead of parking meters made it look different from all the other towns he had driven through. He slowed to a snail's pace, trying not to gawk as he craned his neck to take it all in. He couldn't believe it. There was a furniture store on the corner next to a bakery and a café. "Impossible!" he murmured, "Is that a Bed and Breakfast place?" He hoped so. He might need a place to stay if his father threw him out.

He was more shocked to notice a few of the business had Christmas decorations, including colored lights. The traditional Amish never used electricity and only used items from nature for decorating. He recalled the wreaths of pine branches his mother made, and the pine cones, holly branches and wild nuts his older brothers would bring home. Thinking of how much he had loved helping to arrange the items around the house for the holiday decorating, made him feel nostalgic.

A horde of heavily bearded Amish farmers were nursing steaming cups of coffee in the bakery. It seemed to be the gathering spot of choice now, much like the old general store used to be. They were there, he knew, warming their hands before heading out to clear the streets. Such chores had always been community projects and an amazing amount of work could be accomplished in a short period of time. While the men worked their wives would band together to prepare a community dinner.

He watched the men milling around from the safety of his car. The desire for a hot cup of coffee was tempting but the fear that he might run into someone he knew kept him behind the wheel. Maybe later, he promised himself. Right now the thought of facing the horde of stern bearded elders made him feel like a boy again. As it was, a dozen pair of eyes followed his movements as he shifted gears and made his way slowly through town. Cars were still few and far between. Once those men got wind of why he was here the news would travel fast. The Amish grapevine could put telecommunications systems to shame.

The Barnhart house was two miles out of town on the left. He wondered if the children still called it the 'old house on the hill' and gathered there to play. The hill wasn't as steep as he remembered, but high enough for sledding and rambunctious games of tag. He frowned, not sure he wanted to tackle an unplowed driveway, even with 4-wheel drive.

Instead he parked at the bottom of the driveway, snatched up his black medical bag, and hoisted his laptop carrier onto his shoulder. Someone was here. He followed small fresh footprints up the curve of the drive to the front porch.

The porch had been swept clean and was in good repair, his father had always been meticulous about home maintenance. Like the good son he had always been he stomped his feet to knock the wet snow off his boots before raising his fist to knock on the door.

A loud crash and a yelp sounded from just inside the door. His reluctance to cross the threshold forgotten, he flung open the door. A thin disheveled man dressed only in long johns took a wobbly step toward the young woman crouched behind the kitchen table, a piece of ceramic piercing the soft skin of her forearm. He watched her tear off her apron to staunch the flow of blood before moving forward to intervene. Through the entire episode she continued to speak in a calm voice hoping to sooth the raving apparition. "Hiram," she crooned softly. "It's Sarah. I'm here for you. Everything is going to be okay. Sit down now and I'll bring you something cool to drink."

Matt rushed toward his *dat* and threw his arms out to catch him just as he pitched forward. His eyes were frantic as he struck out repeatedly and placed a well-aimed kick against Matt's knee that nearly bowled him over. The years fell away. Hiram was still as strong as an ox.

He nodded at his medical bag. "There's a syringe with a sedative in there. It's quite mild but might help relax him a bit. Can you give him this if I can hold him still?"

She opened the bag and looked at the syringe. Stammering she said, "I don't know. I have practiced a few times at school but I've never given a shot to real person before."

"It's the same principle, go ahead." he said as he tightened his grip and pinned Hiram's flailing limbs snuggly against his body. It took considerable effort. The man he barely recognized as his father was stronger than he looked. Hiram Barnhart struggled until tears ran down his face. "Who are you?" he gasped.

Sarah quickly emptied the syringe into Hiram's bare buttock. The skin was considerably softer than the orange she had practiced on at school but she didn't have time to be scared. Hiram sagged against Matt, whispering again, "Who are you?"

Matt made eye contact and spoke softly in the soft no nonsense voice that he had perfected over the years. "I am here to see you. Relax now, sit down and let me help you." Matt crab walked the old man backward toward the couch and eased him back into the cushions. He reached down to pick up the patterned quilt that had fallen to the floor. He recognized it as one that his *mamm* had made many years ago. It brought back memories, some of them good memories, of a time long before things had gone so terribly wrong. His fingers caressed the soft material. It had been his quilt, a quilt that he had to leave behind when he fled into the night. His *mamm* had been a skilled needlewoman and he remembered watching her piece the fabric squares together. She had asked him what colors he wanted and he had chosen shades of cream and brown. The end result was striking, and he had loved it. He swallowed, overcome with an unbearable feeling of sadness.

A soft moan from Hiram's lips brought Matt out of his reverie and he finished his task. Only when assured that his patient was resting quietly did he turn to Sarah, actually seeing her for the first time. At thirteen she had been tall and thin with big feet and a distinct inability to control her movements. The ugly duckling, not that she had ever been ugly, has turned into a very lovely swan. He caught his breath, unable to take his eyes off from her, and whispered, "Sarah?"

"You came! Oh, thank God, you came." She cried, throwing her arms around him and giving him a big hug before drawing back. "I'm sorry, I'm getting blood all over you." Matt found he that he didn't mind at all but he carefully removed the syringe from her fingers and grabbed at the wadded up apron before it hit the floor. The wound looked quite deep and he wouldn't have been surprised if she had fainted dead away. He slid his arm around her and guided her toward the kitchen sink. She didn't falter until she turned toward him. He felt her body stiffen when she noticed the misshapen ear and the thin scar that extended down the side of his neck. He was used to this reaction but it still bothered him. He ducked his head but didn't move when she reached out to touch his face. "I'm sorry," she murmured. "Perhaps if I had been more skilled I could have..."

He grabbed her hand, "It wasn't your fault Sarah. The wound was infected and short of plastic surgery they were unable to repair it. It doesn't hurt and I can hear well enough."

She shrugged and teased gently, "You could hide behind a beard if you *vanted* to but not because you *vould vant* to hide your face, it's a nice face." He felt his heartbeat accelerate in a most alarming fashion as her fingers traced the pattern formed by the scar tissue. He took a deep breath to steady his nerves as she grasped the edge of the sink to steady herself, but not before he heard her whisper, "I am so glad that you are here."

"And not a minute too soon," he forced himself to look away from her face and focused on her arm. The wound was no longer bleeding but the jagged tear was deep and raw. "I'm sorry, has he been this way before?"

She shook her head. "No, he is usually quite docile. I must have done something to upset him."

He frowned, shaking his head thoughtfully. "You can help me. Run cool water over the wound to make sure there isn't any glass stuck in it. I'll clear off the table so we have a workspace and we will see what we can do."

Sarah seemed to appreciate his take-charge attitude. He smiled encouragingly as she rolled up her sleeves and started cleaning the wound. "Skin tears and gashes are common occurrences at the retirement community where I work," she explained.

Matt nodded. He was glad that she would not collapse on him as one patient collapsing was enough. He forced his eyes away from her face and returned to cleaning up the glass and scrubbing the table. Working with sunlight as the only light source was going to be challenging. He fished a sterile towel out of his medical bag and took a second look at the contents. He usually just carried the essentials but someone, most likely Junie, had filled his bag with everything she could think of that a young trauma surgeon might need out in the field.

"What's so funny?" Sarah asked, puzzled by the expression on his face.

He opened the bag wide so she could see inside. "A medical bag usually just contains a few essentials, but this looks like a good fairy was extra generous."

He positioned his chair so that the sunlight illuminated the jagged gash. It looked painful but she had scrubbed her arm until it glowed pink and clean.

"Her name is June, Junie," he smiled, trying to distract Sarah as he daubed at the wound with an antiseptic solution and injected a numbing agent to dull the pain. "She was, and still is, in charge of one of the largest ER's in the city, and a dear friend. I'm not sure, "he paused, "what would have happened to me if she hadn't used her influence to help save a very sick young boy fourteen years ago."

"I'd like to hear that story," Sarah said. She watched in fascination as he arranged clamps and packages of thread (they were called sutures, she remembered) onto the prepared sterile towel.

Under the right circumstances he had been known to sew a fine seam, so fine in fact that he had often been teased by other residents in his rotation. He hoped so as he didn't want Sarah to have a scar from this misadventure. "Relax," he said softly as he waited for the numbing agent to take effect. "Don't look, if it bothers you. You can close your eyes and take some slow deep breaths." He kept talking in his effort to calm her fears as he closed the gash with layers of tiny stitches.

"You sew a fine seam, doctor. Your mother *vould* be proud." She held her arm out to admire his handiwork before he covered the wound with gauze and wrapped a bandage securely around her arm.

"She was a fine seamstress. I loved watching her sew. The stitches were so small and even that you could hardly see them." Matt glanced shyly at Sarah, feeling reluctant to let go of the soft firm arm that he cradled in both hands. "I noticed that you watched every move and that you handled the syringe quite expertly for an Amish frau. Are you just fascinated with blood and gore or do your interests go beyond that?"

"I *vork* as a nursing assistant at the Tipton Retirement Center and I've taken a few nursing classes at the community college."

"The community is more liberal than it used to be." He stated as a fact. "What does your husband have to say about that?"

"We've had to change with the times. Many women *vork* and even have their own businesses now. I am my own woman and there is no husband."

"As beautiful as you are? I find that hard to believe." He felt an unexplained rush of relief, but he dropped his gaze to fiddle with the bandage instead of meeting her eyes.

Sarah flushed, obviously pleased by his words but she kept her eyes downcast as she spilled out her story. "*Dat* died unexpectedly ten years ago and *grossmamm* came to live *vith* us. My income is necessary if we *vant* to keep our home. The years went by quick-ly," she shrugged. "I was too busy to notice. Now it is too late." She bobbed slightly as she got to her feet, not quite as steady as she pretended to be. "If you could find me an aspirin or something in that bag of yours I think I might be able to fill you in on *vhat* has happened since you left."

Matt stood as she started to draw away, sorry that the moment was over. Sarah seemed to regain her composure as she busied herself around the kitchen. She still wore a traditional Amish dress and a white head cover. He marveled at the grace and simplicity. He had a dozen questions, but knew he had no right to ask them. He wasn't one of them anymore. Instead he gathered up the tools of his trade to put them aside for cleaning and tossed everything else in the garbage along with the last shards of glass from his *dat's* maelstrom. Sarah took the duster from his hand, "*Danki*, thank you Matt, I could have gotten that."

A smile touched his lips, "I have lived with a crusty old bachelor all these years and I've gotten quite good at cleaning up my own messes." He changed the subject. "You said my father had never been violent before. This wasn't because of me was it?"

Sarah shook her head no. "He is usually quite docile. A bad headache I suspect, he gets them often but he has never been like this." She sighed, "He didn't know you *vere* coming – I didn't know you *vere* coming. I mean, I hoped, but I didn't even know if my letter *vould* find you."

"I am sorry that I wasn't better at keeping in touch. At first I kept a low profile because I was afraid someone would come and drag me back, then when I started college, and later medical school, I was so busy that I barely had time to think."

"I understand, Matt. I wouldn't have told anyone where you *vere*, but I'm sure that the postman would have noticed and mentioned it to someone. I missed you though," her voice trailed off.

"You always did make excuses for me Sarah. Thank you for that, but it is time for me to man-up and stop being a frightened little boy."

He tipped two white tablets into her palm, "take these and call me in the morning."

"Call you in the morning?" she recited somberly, a puzzled expression on her face.

"Sorry, just a little medical humor," he shrugged. "Sit down Sarah. Let me know when the coffee is ready. I was going to stop in town for a cup this morning but I didn't want to chance running into anyone I might know."

Matt walked over to check on his sleeping patient. The sedative had erased the troubled crease between Hiram's bushy brows and he looked almost peaceful. Matt wouldn't have recognized his *dat* if he had seen him anywhere else. The years had not been kind.

He reached down to pick up the rumpled quilt that once again been kicked to the floor. His father had never been what you could call a nice man, but he had never been violent either, until that fateful night. "I wonder," Matt thought out loud as he returned to the stove, "what caused him to lose control over his life. Is this coffee done?" he picked up a hot mat to deal with the coffee pot that was all but spewing its contents onto the stove top, "It's looks pretty strong."

"It's good," Sarah said moving to get up from her chair.

"Allow me," he said pouring coffee into two cups and carrying them to the table. "Do you still use cream and sugar?" When they were children they had been allowed to drink a splash of coffee doused liberally with cream and sugar. It had made them feel quite grown up.

Sarah smiled as if the same thought had crossed her mind. "I'm quite grown up now and I am allowed to drink it black."

He laughed. "Me too, I prefer fresh-drip coffee but this doesn't look half bad." Matt set the two cups on the table before settling into a hand-crafted chair. "We need to talk, but I understand if you want to wait until you feel a little better."

"I'm okay. I'm glad you're here. I know this is hard for you, but I didn't know *vhat* else to do." She picked up the steaming cup and made a face as she took a sip, "It's a little on the strong side."

He followed her example and took a careful sip. It was strong indeed, strong enough to knock his socks off. "I'm glad you wrote. You shouldn't have to deal with all of this. This is my family. I always knew that I would have to come back and face my past sooner or later." He shook his head, "Your letter just made it happen sooner rather than later."

"I expected you to be distant or angry but I'm not getting that feeling about you," she looked up at him.

He shrugged, "I stopped being angry a long time ago. That beating changed my life. I was confused and angry for a long time, but it all turned out for the best. You were the one that helped me most Sarah. You were there for me when I needed you most, and I've treated you shabbily."

He looked down at her hands, capable hands, he thought. "Your words of encouragement helped me put one foot in front of the other until I made it to Tipton. As luck would have it a bus to the city pulled in just as I got there and the coins that you pressed into my hand were enough to get me to the city. By the time I got there I was so sick that I just wanted to die. Luckily a Good Samaritan found me huddled in front of the bus station, and not only got me into the ER but welcomed me into his home. I was believably happy there Sarah. The only one I really missed was you."

"I'm glad you found happiness Matthew. I'm not sure I understood what was going on up here but I do know that Hiram made your life miserable. Your *mamm* missed you though, every day of her life."

Matt stared down at his cup mumbling "Not enough to stand up to him, but I do understand now that it wasn't her fault either. It's just the way it was back then." He lifted his cup to clink it against hers in a silent toast. "I'm going to need your help to evaluate the situation and come up with a plan."

"I'll do anything I can," she stammered timidly. "Do you think he is bi-polar or something?"

~ 89 ~

He cocked his head and gave her a thoughtful look. "Why would you think that?"

"I'm sorry; perhaps I stepped out of bounds." Sarah spoke apologetically as if afraid that her words might offend him.

"No, no, please don't apologize. Observation is a keen diagnostic tool." He stroked his chin thoughtfully. "Obviously you've seen something that makes you think beyond 'mean old man.'"

"He wasn't always like that. People talk. They remember *vhat* he *vas* like as a young man and as a young adult, but no one understands who he is today."

Matt nodded, listening carefully to her words before adding, "I thought it was my fault, something I did, but now I wonder."

"Children always think it is their fault," Sarah said soberly, "but this cannot be so, a child is innocent unless taught to be otherwise." she sighed.

"My therapist said the same thing, but somehow I like hearing it from you better. When did you become so wise?" He wanted to reach out and touch her face but restrained himself. He didn't want to frighten her.

"Spinsters have a lot of time to read," she said dryly, "now, tell me *vhat* you think."

"You may be right. A personality disorder, early dementia or even a slow growing brain tumor are all within the realm of possibilities. I did a neurology rotation and I know enough to know that I need a second opinion to conform my suspicions. I do think something is going on but I'm not sure what. I shouldn't have run away. I gave up on him."

"You had to save yourself," Sarah said with the same self-assured manner she had exhibited as cheeky teenager. "If you weren't a doctor you wouldn't have been able to help him anyway."

Matt nodded. "You are right of course," thinking once again that she was wise beyond her years. "Tell me everything you can about his behavior, as far back as you can remember."

She took a deep breath. "Do you mind if we eat something first. I'm still a little shaky and I feel like I've been up forever."

"I could eat too. Something smells good. When did you have time to cook?"

"Your *dat* refuses to let anyone from the community come into the house but the ladies have banned together to shop and send food every day. I put the hot dish in the oven before he woke up and started throwing dishes at me."

"He's lucky you didn't head for the door."

"I might have if you hadn't arrived *vhen* you did."

Matt grinned, touched by her admission. "Well, I'm glad you didn't. I would have had to pop him one to gain control."

Sarah deposited two plates onto the table both filled with generous portions of a savory ground beef casserole flanked by thick slices of buttered bread.

"I'd forgotten how good a home cooked meal tasted. Max and I usually ate at the hospital cafeteria or heated something in the microwave."

"No dates and fancy restaurants?" she teased.

He snorted. "Once in a while, but most of the women I dated were either dieting or on such restricted diets that it wasn't exactly a culinary delight."

"Is that *vhy* you are so thin?"

"Thin? I haven't paid much attention. The ladies at the hospital cafeteria made sure I didn't starve though."

When they had finished Matt stacked the empty dishes and stood to carry them to sink.

"You don't have to do that," she said struggling to get to her feet.

He touched her shoulder gently. "Sit down. I don't want you to get your bandage wet. We'll just let them soak while we talk. Is there something sweet to nibble on around here?"

"You always did have a sweet tooth. There are some of my *mamm's* cookies in the basket there. She bakes every morning to sell at the restaurant in town."

"The Cornucopia on Main Street?"

"You know of the Cornucopia?"

"I drove past it this morning. I think every man in town was in there drinking coffee. It seems to be quite the gathering spot." Matt refilled their coffee cups and carried them back to the table.

Sarah took a tin of cookies out of the huge basket that she had toted up the hill that morning, "They eat a lot of cookies."

"Can't say I blame them," he mumbled around a mouthful of gingersnap crumbs, your mom is a genius in the kitchen."

"It has been hard on her since *dat* died. I know she doesn't begrudge taking care of *grossmamm* but she craves grown up company. She is happier now that she has a mission. She thinks she is saving me from myself." Sarah broke her cookie in half and dunked the smaller portion into her coffee cup. "I didn't see much of your family after you left. They seemed to withdraw from the community except for the occasional trip to the general store. Until your *mamm* died I don't think I actually saw Hiram more than a dozen times over the years. Bishop Troyer tried to draw him back into the community but he refused everyone's efforts."

"It's hard to take care of someone who doesn't want to be taken care of. The thought of 'for your own good' goes just so far. We see a lot of that in the medical community." Matt admitted.

"Yes. We see that *vith* the 'old dears' in the Retirement Center too. Hiram refused to let the community help him. After your *mamm* died. I found him passed out in the yard one day last fall, nearly dead from hypothermia. Until today he hasn't fussed about my regular visits. He never did talk much but he *vould* eat the food I brought, and he didn't throw me out. This morning was different. He stood up *vhen* I was putting the casserole in the oven, clutched his head, and just went crazy."

"You were very kind; you could have called 911 and they would have admitted him to a psychiatric unit."

"I didn't *vant* to leave him," she stammered, "and I didn't have my work phone *vith* me."

"Sorry. I forgot about the no phone rule. Boy, it has been a long time hasn't it?" He sat down across from Sarah again, "So far we've isolated depression, anxiety, mood swings and severe headaches which have increased gradually over the years."

"Yes, until a few months ago he *vas* still able to work, but lately he is always in bed *vhen* I get here. He eats, but doesn't clean up or even get dressed now."

"Good observations, I appreciate that and will do an examination when he wakes up and then I want to talk to some of my neurology professors."

"Does that mean that it might be something other than 'personality disorder'?"

"I'm not ruling anything out but I need to know a lot more before I can be sure. In ER we often have to make snap decisions but this may have been ongoing for many years. Does that make sense to you?"

"I think so. You don't want to make a diagnosis first and then manipulate the symptoms to make your case."

He stood up abruptly. "You've been doing more than a little reading."

She shrugged. "I have an inquiring mind."

"You do indeed. Why don't you let me take you home. I'll write a note excusing you from work for a few days."

"That won't be necessary. I am off until Sunday."

"Good. Is there anywhere closer than Tipton where I can get internet access? I'm going to do some research and make some phone calls but I hate leaving him alone."

"There are a half dozen coffee shops and the library in Tipton but you could check with the proprietor of the Lake View Bed and Breakfast right here in town too. I'll stay with Hiram while you are out."

"You'd still do that, after this morning?"

She smiled gently, "I never could say no to you, besides he looks pretty harmless right now."

Matt drove Sarah to the door of her house, the same house she had lived in all of her life. Her *mamm* threw open the door and glared at Matt in confusion. "Who is this? *Vhy* did you come home in a car? Is everything alright?"

Sarah touched her *mamm's* arm, trying to hide her bandaged arm under her cloak. "It's okay *mamm*. *Ve* had a little emergency. Matt needs me to stay with his *dat* while he goes into town. I thought maybe you *vould* like to help me."

"Matt? Little Matt?" Her expression softened to one of wonder." Oh my goodness. Come in child, and let me look at you."

Matt smiled at her, surprised that she remembered him, but stepped back. "It's good to see you, but we are in a hurry and I don't want to leave my *dat* alone today. Sarah has hurt her arm so I don't want her to use it much. Your help would be much appreciated."

Abigail quickly agreed, always glad to be of help. She grabbed her coat and the two women accompanied him to Hiram's house and filed through the door without giving Matt a backwards glance. He wasn't quite ready to feed the gossip mill but he knew it was out of his hands now.

The sedative had already started to wear off and Hiram was up, scrawny legs once again entangled in the old quilt. He frowned, bleary eyed trying to focus on the young man standing in front of him. His voice thick and raspy, "Who in the hell are you?"

Matt took a deep breath and waved Abigail off, "I'll handle it." He hung his jacket on the peg behind the door and moved slowly toward the couch. Hiram gave no indication that he actually recognized Matt as he staggered to his feet. "Help me to the bathroom or I'll mess all over the floor."

It was a start, Matt thought, as he supported his *dat* to the bathroom. The fact that he recognized that he needed help was a good sign. The short walk told the doctor in Matt a lot. For one thing the man was too unsteady on his feet to stay in the house alone if any sedation was going to be involved. Matt left the old man in the bathroom and returned to straighten the makeshift bed.

He pulled clean night clothes out of the laundry basket of neatly folded clothes and laid them on the worn couch. Obviously, the village ladies had been doing Hiram's laundry too. He hoped the pompous old fool appreciated their efforts.

Matt slipped easily into his professional persona. When his father had finished in the bathroom, he stood back to observe and assess Hiram's movements instead of offering to dress him. A wave of compassion touched his heart and he wanted to put his arms around the old man to comfort him. At the same time he didn't want to trigger the agitation either. It was important that both men remained calm if he was going to be able to examine his father. Matt pulled a chair from the kitchen over to the couch and sat down, speaking in what his patients referred to as his 'doctor voice'. "I am your doctor Hiram, and between the two of us we are going to figure out why you have this problem with headaches and balance."

He sensed that Hiram's mind was already drifting away from him. He called him back to attention by reverting to something he could understand. "Would you like something to eat before we start? The ladies have a very tasty casserole in the oven."

Hiram wrinkled his brow and thought for a full minute before he responded, "*Ja*, I could eat."

Matt crushed a sedative tablet and mixed it into a serving of the hot dish left warming in the oven before he carried it over to the couch sat it down on the nightstand.

Hiram took a few hearty bites. "It's good."

"You have friends in the community, Hiram, even though you have seen fit to shut them out."

"*Vhere's* the girl?" he demanded gruffly, not noticing the two women bustling around in the kitchen.

"You don't remember?" Matt inquired.

Hiram frowned, obviously not remembering his earlier outburst.

"You threw dishes at her and hurt her rather badly this morning. I had to stitch her arm, but she has kindly offered to stay with you until you feel better."

Hiram finished the meal before he spoke again. "I'm sorry, I don't know *vhy* I did that. My head hurt so badly I just *vanted* to lash out."

"Does it hurt right now?"

"It never goes away completely but it isn't too bad right now."

"Good. I want to examine you but I need you to stay with me. No yelling, no screaming and no striking out. Do you think you can do that?

"I'll try," he said, looking up at Matt. "Do I know you?"

"We'll talk about that later, right now just listen to my voice and know that I want to help you." He knew the importance of maintaining a calm confident demeanor to elicit cooperation from an unstable patient. "Look at me." he commanded softly, tilting Hiram's head up so he that he could do a comprehensive neurological examination. He saved the most difficult question until last, "How long have you had these headaches and mood swings?"

"As long as I can remember but they are worse now. I can't stand much more of this." His voiced faded out as the medication took effect and he offered little resistance as Matt swung his legs up onto the coach and covered him the quilt.

Matt noticed that Abigail and Sarah were both staring and he smiled reassuringly. "He should sleep now. I've given him a little more of the sedative but if you feel uncomfortable watching him I won't go."

Sarah offered him her cell phone. "If you *vill* program your number into my work phone so that I can reach you, we'll stay."

"I thought you didn't use cell phones?" he asked as he took the small phone from her hand.

"*Ve* don't," she stammered," but the place I work at insists that all staff members carry one in case they need to get a hold of us. It belongs to them."

"Good, I feel better about leaving. I promise not to be gone long. I just need to do get on-line to do some reading and talk to a few specialists."

"*Ve'll* stay. Hiram won't stand a chance with two strong women *vanting* to take care of him." Abigail nodded her head in agreement.

"A couple of hours max. Call me if you have trouble. I'll be right here." He gave Sarah her phone back and slipped his back into his pocket. He hoped that he wasn't compromising Sarah's principles too badly. He had lived in the 'world' for so long now that it was adjustment even to walk into a room that didn't have electricity. Hiram was snoring gently but Matt paused to explain to the man that he was leaving for a while but that Sarah would be there if he needed anything. "I want you to behave yourself," he said using his best doctor voice. The only answer was a loud snort.

The library in Tipton was easy to find and possessed every modern amenity. A helpful librarian ferreted out a quiet corner where he could work without interruption. Twenty minutes on the internet and a long conversation with Phil, a buddy specializing in Neurology, confirmed most of Matt's suspicions. He followed up on Phil's advice to contact one of their instructors who practiced in Tipton now. Matt remembered Doctor Rodney Lewis, the 'show no fear' guy who had delighted in tormenting his students.

Matt waited fifteen minutes before he placed a call to Dr. Lewis. Phil, true to his word, had paved the way by contacting the specialist first. Dr. Lewis answered the phone on the first ring and told Matt he would be happy to help. "I'll tell you what," he offered, "I have an appointment out that way that way later this afternoon so I can stop by on the way home. I know where Moss Lake is so it's no problem. Are the roads drivable?"

"No problem if you have 4-wheel drive. The men in town have been out clearing the streets since dawn."

"Great! I'll see you later then," the doctor replied.

As he hung up, Matt couldn't believe how quickly things were coming together. A neurologist willing to make a house call would have been unheard of anywhere else. Small town living might not be such a bad idea after all.

Tipton had grown considerably in the last fourteen years. A library, a hospital and half dozen stoplights on Main Street alone constituted a big city is this part of the world. He would love to stay and explore the town but he promised Sarah that he wouldn't be gone long.

He stopped at the hardware store for a deluxe model Coleman lantern and stocked up on extra batteries. Dr. Lewis was going to need more than a kerosene lamp to conduct a thorough examination, and he would probably like a good cup of coffee. A popular coffee shop sold him a French Press coffee maker, which did not require electricity, and a bag of fresh ground beans. Even bachelors had to have a few amenities, didn't they?

The two women had tidied the kitchen and gathered up soiled linens to take with them by the time he arrived back at the farm house. The door to his old room was open and he could see they had stripped the bed and put on fresh linens so that he would have a place to sleep tonight.

"I thought I told you to rest." He started to scold but Sarah's scowl told him to back off, so instead he mouthed, "Thank you."

Abigail looked back and forth and smiled thoughtfully before adding, "There are sandwich ingredients in the refrigerator, if you *vant* to eat later on." At least his *dat* had a propane refrigerator, although most other amenities seemed to be lacking.

Sarah touched him gently on the arm. "You keep telling me to rest, but you are the one needing sleep."

He looked over at Hiram who was snoring peacefully. "I have a specialist dropping by to see him later this afternoon. I don't want to sedate him again until after the examination but I will sleep after that." He paused, "thank you for getting my room ready."

She nodded. "I *vill* stay if you *vill* take *mamm* home. I should be here in case the doctor has questions." She shook her finger at him when he started to protest. Once again she was in charge; just as she had been fourteen years ago and he knew better than to argue. He nodded his agreement and bundled Abigail out of the door before she could protest.

Sarah settled into the big rocking chair by the window and opened her book to read. She barely glanced up when Matt returned. She did lift her hand to wave him toward the bedroom, "I'll wake you *vhen* your colleague gets here." He was too tired to argue. Ten minutes later he was stretched out under the covers in the Spartan room of his youth. The bedding smelled like fresh air and sunshine, the quilt was the same one that had been on his bed the night he left.

He slept soundlessly until a loud pounding at the door jarred him awake. He staggered to his feet and made his way into the kitchen, not at all surprised to find Sarah sound asleep at the kitchen table with her head pillowed in the crook of her arms. She stirred, blinking sleepily as she pushed herself away from the table.

Matt pulled the door open just as two Amish urchins raised their fist to resume their assault on his door. Sarah pushed him aside. "Maria, Marcus, *vhat* are you doing here?"

Six year old Marcus, who must have been the eldest by only a matter of minutes grabbed at Sarah's skirt. "Sarah. Sarah. Come quickly. Levi's hurt."

Sarah snatched her coat off the peg behind the door and struggled into it as she hurried after the children. Matt staggered back to the bedroom to grab his fleece jacket and boots to follow her outside and see what was going on.

Six year old Levi Straussman sat upright against the fence at the bottom of the hill cradling his right arm and sobbing hysterically. Matt knelt down in the snow beside the boy and assessed the damage. He put on his doctor face while soothing the boy's fears and it worked like magic. The boy hiccoughed gently and let Matt wipe away his tears as he scooped him up in his arms and carried him to the house.

Sarah turned to the twins, "Can one of you go and get Levi's *mamm* and bring her back up here?" The two nodded and took off at a dead run.

Matt carried Levi into the kitchen and perched him on the edge of the table. He supported the boy's shoulder and his elbow before he tugged as gently as he could. "Ouch. Ouch. Ouch." Levi yelled. "It hurts!"

Matt gave him a hug. "I'm sorry, but it doesn't hurt now does it?"

The boy sniveled but stopped yelling to think about it for a minute. "No," he whispered.

"You *vere* very brave." Sarah crooned as she scooped him up in her arms and carried him to the rocking chair. "Your *mamm* is going to be so proud of you."

Levi's *mamm*, a frightened young Amish woman with large eyes and *kapp* askew, rushed into the room. "*Vhat* happened?"

"Levi crashed into the fence with his sled and dislocated his shoulder. He is going to be okay. He will be sore for a few days, but if you give me your scarf I'll make a little sling for him to wear as it will remind him to hold his arm still." She gave him her scarf, hesitatingly, and with a few twists and knots turned it into an old-fashioned sling. "Take him home now, settle him down on the couch, and give him a cookie. I'll be right up here if you need me."

Martha Straussman looked at him her heart in her eyes, too frightened to speak. Matt smiled sympathetically. "He will be fine." He found he rather liked the idea of being able to comfort his patients instead of sending them off to someone else. He was beginning to appreciate why Max enjoyed his family practice so much.

Sarah nodded and took over. She draped Levi's jacket over his shoulders and put her arms around him. "Come," she said quietly, "let's get you home."

"Does he need to see a doctor," Martha whispered to Sarah as she followed her out into the cold.

Sarah shook her head no, "Matt *is* a doctor and if he says Levi *vill* be fine, he *vill* be fine."

Sarah returned to find Matt at the stove pouring boiling water into the French Press he had purchased in town. He pushed the plunger down firmly releasing the tantalizing aroma of strong fresh coffee into the air. "I am glad you *vere* here," she said, "Dr. Anderson died a year ago so we haven't had a family doctor anywhere near in some time."

"It was nothing. I'm glad I could help."

"That was a good thing you did. Martha *vants* to know *vhat* she can do to repay you." Sarah said gravely.

"Not a thing. He was hurt on *dat's* property. If we were anywhere else we would have to be worried that they would sue us. Besides, it's the least I could do."

"Once the word gets out you are going to be besieged with patients."

"The way the community has pitched in to help my *dat* a little medical advice is a small price to pay."

Sarah sat down and accepted the cup of coffee from him, sighing in appreciation. "I don't know about that," she said thoughtfully, "the boy I knew *vas* pretty wonderful."

A faint smile touched the corner of Matt's mouth as he looked around him. This house where he grew up appeared smaller and more worn, but it was clean and he was amazed to see simple Amish Christmas decorations. "Sarah, you are incredible. Where do you find the time to keep this place so clean and you even decorated!"

Sarah blushed at his praise, "Once I got the place cleaned up, it *vas* easy to maintain as your *dat* is usually docile, and the *kinner* brought in the decorations for me." She stammered, "I thought it might help Hiram feel better."

There was a knock on the door and Matt walked over to answer it. Dr. Lewis stood there. He looked more approachable in dark slacks and sweater than Matt remembered but the man was still all business. He shrugged out of his car coat and offered his hand. "Good to see you Dr. Barnhart," He looked around, trying to take everything in, before focusing on his patient. "Amish?" he questioned.

"My father is Amish, yes. I hope the battery-operated lights will be sufficient for you. This," he said, drawing Sarah to his side, "is Sarah. She has known our patient for years and has spent more time with him of late than anyone else."

He smiled and nodded to Sarah. "Good to meet you. I think I have everything with me that I will need but stand by in case I have any questions. If your suspicions are correct, Matt, as I suspect they might be, we'll have to take him in for some scans."

"Who is Dr. Lewis?" Sarah whispered as she dropped into her chair beside Matt.

"Dr. Lewis headed up the Neurology Department at the hospital when I was a student. He moved back home to Tipton when his wife was diagnosed with MS and has a private practice in the Tri-City area now. The neurologist at the University Hospital referred me to him and he agreed to see *dat*."

"Do you think your *dat* has a brain tumor?" Sarah asked.

Matt was amazed at how quickly Sarah grasped what was going on. "It certainly has to be ruled out, but we'll see. *Dat* was never an easy man to live with but he wasn't rude and disorderly. He was good to my *mamm* but we children were just too much for him to handle."

They sat back, watching Dr. Lewis as he worked, admiring the way the irritable Hiram responded to the man's calm confident manner.

"Never show fear," he would tell all of the new interns. "Pretend that you know what you are doing, even if you don't." It was good advice, but the trick was exuding confidence without appearing arrogant, not an easy task.

Dr. Lewis finished up his examination and poured himself a cup of coffee before walking over to the table and settling into one of the hardwood chairs. "Stop looking so worried. I agree with your initial assessment Matt, but we will need to do some scans to confirm. It could be a meningioma, a slow-growing benign, tumor. Because they are slow growing they can reach a substantial size before any symptoms are present. I called the hospital and scheduled him for 10:00 in the morning. Give him a sedative before bringing him. If he gives you any trouble, call an ambulance."

"Yes, sir, we'll be there. Thank you. I am grateful that you are willing to take the case."

The older doctor smiled at the earnest young man standing before him, "the pleasure is all mine." He nodded to Sarah but knew enough about the Amish to refrain from offering his hand. "It was nice to meet you too young lady. Your care and the history that you compiled may save Hiram's life." He smiled warmly, "Matt and Hiram are both lucky to have you in their lives."

Sarah blushed with pleasure, glad that she had been able to help. "The whole community came together to help. I *vas* the only one he would allow in the house."

"It's not unusual for people with pressure in this area of the brain to feel anxious and paranoid. It would be good if both of you could accompany him tomorrow. We need maximum cooperation from our patient. Matt, does he seem know who you are?"

"I don't think so. I didn't want to chance agitating him by bringing up old memories. We parted on less than ideal circumstances."

"Probably just as well," he smiled at Matt and said, "Remember, no fear."

"I remember."

Dr. Lewis continued, "He can have nothing to eat or drink after midnight, and if the scan confirms what I think it will, we'll operate tomorrow."

"That soon?" Sarah and Matt echoed each other.

The older doctor nodded, "I know you don't have insurance so we will try to keep the costs down. Not spending extra days in the hospital is one way to do that."

Matt inhaled sharply. He appreciated the practicality. The community would help as able but he knew he would be paying off the surgery for the rest of his life.

The next day Dr. Lewis did not waste any time. The scans confirmed his suspicious and he operated on Hiram the same day.

Afterward, Matt sat beside Hiram's bed all night long. Sleep eluded him as he relived every moment of the last fourteen years. Could a slowly growing tumor really have been responsible for all those years of his father's abnormal behavior?

"Matt." The old man croaked, his lips dried and cracked. "Is that you?"

Mat stood up quickly and set his laptop down on the chair he had just vacated. He didn't speak, not sure if he should answer or not. He nodded slightly instead, "How much do you remember?"

"I drove you all away," he said soberly, turning his head away. "You must hate me."

Matt picked up the cup of ice chips from the bedside table and placed a small spoonful on Hiram's tongue. "I don't hate you. My only regret is that I had to become a doctor to recognize that something might have been wrong. In a sense, it was my fault too."

Hiram shook his head in despair. "You *vere* just a boy. It *vasn't* your job to take care of me," He paused. "I knew I *vasn't* right, even back then, but I *vas* too proud to ask for help. Pride is a sin and I *vas* the greatest sinner of them all." He took a slow, deep breath, "is Sarah here?"

"You like her, huh?" Matt teased. "I sent her to the lounge to rest. Dr. Lewis wants to release you as soon as he is sure that there won't be any swelling. Sarah and I will look after you if you will let us. It is very expensive to stay here."

"I understand, we'll figure out a *vay* to pay."

"I know, but I don't want you to be worried about that now. Dr. Lewis will be pleased to hear that you are awake and remembering things."

At the sound of his name Dr. Lewis stepped into the cubicle, "I heard enough to know that the surgery was a success and the outcome is good." He examined Hiram and announced. "I want to keep you a day or two but you should be able to go directly home with your son. The surgery was relatively minor as the tumor was benign and non-invasive so, while it projected pressure against your brain, I couldn't see much damage."

Hiram nodded his understanding and closed his eyes whispering. "My head doesn't hurt."

Matt followed Dr. Lewis out of the room. "Is everything okay? I suppose the hospital is already wondering how we are going to pay for this?"

"Of course," he shrugged, "but they know that the Amish take care of their own, but perhaps I can help," he took Matt's arm and guided him to a window seat in the waiting room. "I have an idea." Matt knew that Dr. Lewis was famous for his "ideas." He was a very creative man.

Dr. Lewis laughed. "I know that look and I also know that my students had great fun dissecting my "creative ideas," but I didn't always work in places with state-of-the art equipment."

"Let's hear it," Matt said as he dropped into a chair and rubbed weary eyes.

"No charge for my services per se, just a little bit of blackmail. I know you haven't decided what kind of medicine you want to practice yet so perhaps you will be receptive to my idea. Tipton Memorial has plans to upgrade their ER to a first class trauma unit. We could use someone with your experience to help us get the program off the ground. I am on the board and could arrange a free ride on the hospital bill in exchange for your help if you would see fit to give us a year or so of your time." The older doctor paused, allowing Matt time to assimilate his words. "I could promise you enough time to see patients on your own if you want to try private practice."

"Are you serious?" Matt gasped thinking immediately that it might give him time to get to know Sarah again, although the odds were against them. He could live on the fringe but wouldn't be accepted as an Amish doctor and Sarah…would she leave her family and friends?

"I am! Dr. Melrose assures me that you were one of the best trauma residents to rotate through his service. That's high praise coming from him."

"Thank you for your kind words," Matt stammered not really believing what he was hearing. "I think I might like that, but can you give me a few days to settle my *dat* in and give it some thought? So much has happened in the last twenty-four hours that my head is spinning."

"You can take as much time as you need. Take a few weeks and enjoy an old fashioned Amish Christmas. I know at your age a year or two seems like an eternity but we could really use your help." He stood up holding out his hand. "Max is a friend of mine too. I know your story and want you to know that I will understand, whatever your decision."

◇◇◇

Sarah felt disoriented but rested when she woke. She had been dozing in the lounge when one of the nurses took pity on her and offered to let her sleep in one of the on-call rooms. Someone has slipped in while she slept and left a hospital robe and fresh towels on the chair by the door. People were incredibly nice. She managed to shower without getting her bandage wet and twenty minutes later stepped into the hall to make her way back to the Neurology Unit. Matt was sound asleep in the chair beside the bed. She caught her breath as he looked not unlike the teenage boy she had known so well.

A voice speaking from the bed startled her, "Good looking boy don't you think?" It was the first words Hiram had spoken to her in years.

"He is indeed. Do you remember me?" she said softly as she stepped up to the bed.

"Yes." He nodded. You two *vere* best friends all through school. *Ve* thought the two of you might marry one day."

Sarah smiled, not sure what she should say. So much history, so much time had passed.

Hiram reached out and touched the bandage on her arm, "I remember a lot of things, most of them that I'm not very proud of it."

"*Velcome* back," she said gently touching his hand.

Matt stirred and mumbled, "Good Morning."

"Good Morning to you too, she stuttered "It's early yet if you *vant* to go to the on-call room and sleep for a little while. I can sit with your *dat*."

"I actually slept quite well here. Dr. Lewis was in earlier. Everything went well but he wants to keep *dat* here for a day or two for observation."

She nodded and whispered, "He knows who you are."

"I know," he smiled.

"*Vell*, go take a shower and I'll find us a cup of coffee."

"Yes boss." He chuckled, Sarah hadn't changed a bit. "There's an espresso stand in the lobby. Get us both the largest cup of drip coffee you can find, or treat yourself to a latte if you would like." He handed her a $20 bill and ducked out of the room only to come back a few second later to say, "Maybe a breakfast sandwich too."

Hiram peered at him out from under his bandages. "Bring one for me too. I am not going to eat another bite of that wiggly green stuff that they keep trying to feed me."

"I'll bring you steak as soon as Dr. Lewis says okay."

"It's okay with me," Dr. Lewis bellowed from the doorway. "You can go home in a day or two." He walked over to the bed and peered into Hiram's pupils with his pen light and nodded in satisfaction. "As I said earlier, the tumor was benign and we got it all. Matt and Sarah have promised to take good care of you and it would be a shame to spend Christmas here."

"Thanks Dr. Lewis," Matt said from the doorway. "I'll talk to you in a few days."

Hiram's day nurse introduced herself as Lilly. "I'll be in here with Mr. Barnhart for about a half an hour. Go ahead and get some breakfast. I'll find something a little more palatable for my patient."

Matt waited until they were seated in the cafeteria before he turned to Sarah. "Dr. Lewis has offered me a position here to help set up a new trauma unit. He would like me to commit for year. Do you think I should do it?"

"You are asking my opinion?" she studied his face looking for a clue but his expression was bland. "*Vhy* are you asking me?"

"I've always valued your opinion, Sarah."

She looked down at her plate and pretended that her sandwich was the most interesting thing in the world to her. "*Vould* it be so terrible to stay here?"

"I shouldn't refuse," he shrugged. "It will obliterate the cost of *dat's* surgery and hospitalization, and give me an excuse to hang around for a year. I was wondering, if I said yes," he paused, trying to find the right words, "would you consider working part time for me? Dr. Lewis said I would have time to open a small practice on my own if I wanted to. I think I might like that, but I couldn't do it alone." He studied her face, trying to gauge her thoughts, but she refused to look up. Finally Matt could not handle the suspense any longer. "Oh for heaven's sake, Sarah, stop fiddling with your sandwich and look at me."

Startled, she looked up. The thought of working with Matt was tempting, but was she reading too much into his offer? "I already have a job, and I owe them tuition for the classes I've taken."

"I could take care of that. You could go to school full time if you would like, or not."

She frowned, her heart in her eyes as she met his earnest eyes. "*Vhy* would you do that for me?"

Matt, relieved, smiled tenderly at her. "I thought you knew. I've been in love with you since I was thirteen years old."

Sarah looked up, her eyes wide, and breathed a soft, "Oh."

Abigail's Apple Muffin Recipe

1 egg

½ cup of milk

¼ cup of cooking oil

1 cup of grated apples

1 ½ cup of flour

½ cup of sugar

2 teaspoons of baking powder

½ teaspoon of salt

½ teaspoon of cinnamon

¼ teaspoon of allspice

Pre-heat oven to 400° F – Grease the bottom of 12 medium-sized muffin cups – Beat egg then stir in milk and oil – Add and mix in remaining ingredients, just until flour is moistened (batter should be lumpy) – Place batter into muffin cup and top with Crunchy Topping (recipe below) – Bake for 25-30 minutes or until done.

Crunchy Topping: Mix together 1/3 cup of brown sugar, 1/3 cup of finely chopped nuts, ½ teaspoon of cinnamon and ¼ teaspoon of cloves.

About Linda Buroker

Linda Buroker is a retired nurse who worked with the elderly for many years. She became interested in helping seniors age-in-place and now writes a blog on the subject of aging successfully.

She lives in the Pacific NW with her husband and two dogs where she enjoys a good mystery novel, writing and hiking.

Other books by Ms. Buroker:

> Ms. Buroker's first novella was published in New Beginnings, A Collection of Christmas Stories, published by Martin's Muses, December 2014.

> Yesterday, Today and Tomorrow, An Anthology: Ms. Buroker was a contributing author to this anthology.

> Books available on Amazon

Read her blog at: www.lmb.typepad.com/smart_senior

A Christmas Baby

Crystal Linn

Dorcas Stolzfus stumbled into Healthy Alternatives, the local herb shop, her prayer *kapp* askew and her long wool coat buttoned crooked. She was hyperventilating so hard she could barely breathe. Anna McLean, master herbalist and owner of the store, quickly grabbed a small bottle from under the counter and dashed over to Dorcas, guiding her to the closest chair. Anna opened the bottle and poured some contents from the bottle into the lid. Handing it to the young, skinny woman Anna said, "Here, Dorcas drink this. It will help." Once the herbal treatment began to work and the young Amish woman started calming down, Anna encouraged her to take slow deep breaths.

"B-u-t, my b-a-b-y," Dorcas stammered. "He's disappeared!" Once she got the words out, she began to sob again.

Anna reached out to the hysterical Dorcas and placed a gentle yet firm hand on each shoulder. Taking a few slow deep breaths of her own, she sent up a prayer asking for the right words.

"Dorcas," Anna's voice was gentle, "tell me exactly what happened."

The young mother forced herself to take another deep breath, "*Vell*...as you know, the King family has been staying *vith* us *vhile* their house *vas* being repaired from that large tree falling through the roof during our last snow storm." Anna nodded, indicating she knew about the situation and Dorcas continued, "They left this morning to move back into their home. It is also my morning to go *vork,* work, for my *mutter*-in-law, Martha. So I told the King family-ly good-bye and *vent* to Martha's at 7:00 a.m. The Kings planned to leave an hour later. So instead of taking Caleb *vith* me I left him sleep longer since he has this cough and cold. Young Grace Knepp had said she *vould* come over as the King's *vere* leaving." Dorcas paused to take more deep breaths. "At 8:15 a.m. Martha and I heard pounding on the door. *Vhen* I opened it, Grace *vas* standing there in tears. She had told the Kings good-bye then gone upstairs to check on Caleb but he *vas* not in his crib. You know how relia-ble Grace is – Anna please help us!" Dorcas clutched at Anna's hands as tears streamed down her face.

Anna gently untangled her hands from Dorcas' hands as she stood up. Nátanik, Anna's sister-in-law, had left the counter and walked over to join the conversation. She and Anna gave each other an understanding look. The young woman immediately reached in her pocket for her cell phone, pulling at her long black braid as she walked away.

"Dorcas, Nátanik is calling Matthew and I will call Lucas. We will find your baby." Anna sounded more confident than she felt. It was the middle of winter in Montana and unknown dangers lurked in the cold. "You need to go home in case someone finds him and brings him to you." Anna paused, "I'm assuming your husband and Bishop Stolzfus know?"

Dorcas nodded her head, "*Ja*, both men were at my in-laws *vhen* Grace came."

Anna nodded, "Go home, Dorcas, take this bottle with you and take one half of a teaspoon every four hours. It will help keep your calm…"

Dorcas shook her head. "Dorcas," Anna scolded, "it is important to keep calm so you can think and act more clearly. Lucas and Matthew will work with your father-in-law, the bishop, and the rest of the community." Anna sighed mentally but aloud said, "It will be alright."

Dorcas nodded as she stood, "*Danki*, thank you, Anna, I know It *vill*. You and your family are true friends to us Amish."

Anna sighed loud enough for Dorcas to hear, "Remember, I was raised Amish."

Nátanik walked over to Anna as Dorcas turned to walk out of the store, a frown on her dark-complexed face. "Matt is calling Lucas. They will contact the bishop and Dorcas' husband, Samuel.

The men, English, Amish and Kootenai Indian, all gathered together in the Sheriff's office. Ranger, Lucas's dog, half German Shepherd and half Wolf, sat silent by his side. Matt also had his dog with him. The men were visibly upset and, even though they had their difference, they all agreed that a baby was a special gift and Caleb needed found as soon as possible.

Using the map on the wall, the sheriff made a grid and the group divided into teams to cover all of the grid areas. The temperature was dropping and was expected to be well below freezing by night fall.

The Amish men had no issues with riding in the trucks of their English and Kootenai neighbors, after all this was an emergency. Lucas drove Samuel Stolzfus home to get some of the baby's clothing for the dogs to sniff. Tracking in the deep snow would be difficult enough and he wanted the two dogs to have all of the help they could get. Lucas' son, Mark, and Bishop Stolzfus were with them.

The instant Ranger sniffed Caleb's clothes he got all excited as if he recognized the scent and knew where to go. Shaking his head, Lucas gave Ranger the command to go and find. The dog leaped away, happy and confident. The three men and Mark got into the truck and followed the eager canine.

Ranger ran directly home, to the McLean homestead. Lucas turned into his own driveway and shook his head. "What is with this dog?" He spoke more to himself than to the others riding with him. "He never faltered once today in following Caleb's scent."

Ranger dashed into the gigantic horse barn which Lucas and Matt's father had built. Lucas parked the truck in front of the barn and the four of them jumped out and dashed inside. Ranger was standing at the foot of the ladder barking joyfully and wagging his tail. "Ranger, quiet," Lucas commanded. As the men looked at each other, uncertain as to what to think, they heard a child singing above them.

Lucas grabbed a hold of the ladder rungs and was up in the hay loft within seconds. What he saw amazed him. The King twins were nestled in the hay with Caleb, their small bonnets and aprons crooked. The girls were startled at being discovered and Rebecca, the gentler of the two, began to cry. He did not know whether to comfort them or yell at them. He took a deep breath and held it, then let it out slowly as he knew he needed to get control of himself. "Rebecca and Rachel, what are the two of you doing up here with Caleb?"

Rachel, much bolder than Rebecca, spoke, "Baby Jesus was born at Christmas time – and he *vas* killed! Caleb *vas* born at Christmas time and *ve* do not *vant* him to be killed, like Jesus *vas*." She looked up at Lucas as if she was defying him to disagree with her.

As he squatted down, Lucas had to bite his lip to keep from laughing. "Rachel, why did you bring the baby up here, to *my* hay loft?"

"That *vas* easy," the child almost giggled. "Everyone knows your barn is heated and *ve* know all about how Ranger rescued that wolf and her pups last Christmas. *Ve* figured if something happened and *ve* could not make it up here then Ranger *vould* take care of Caleb for us.

Lucas shook his head at her child-like logic. "Rachel, trust me, Caleb will not be killed like Jesus was. Right now we need to get this baby home as he is sick and needs his mother."

He held onto the ladder's sides and called down to the waiting men, "Caleb is here along with the King twins. Mark, would you please call everyone and let them know the baby is safe?

In the McLean living room Dorcas held her first-born son tightly and between her tears of relief she kept asking, "How and *Vhy*?"

Rachel explained how when her parents were loading the last of their belongings into the wagon to return home she and Rebecca tip-toed upstairs and got Caleb out of the crib. "We *vere* very careful *vith* him, and I made sure all of his blankets *vere* wrapped around him tightly, just like *mutter* did *vith* Michael, our little *bruder*." When the adults just shook their heads she stamped her foot and continued. "*Ve* knew that the McLean barn *vas* warm and that Ranger *vould* help. Our house is a long way from here and I thought it *vould* be best to hide Caleb now, since the Stolzfus house is closer." Rachel finished with a sigh and crossed her short pudgy arms in front of herself.

Dorcas shook her head and walk over to sit down by the fireplace where she continued to listen while rocking Caleb in her arms. Anna sat the twins down on her black-leather couch, and sat between them. Placing an arm around each of them, she explained that many babies were born at Christmas time and were gifts from God and were never killed. She concluded by explaining that the story of Jesus was different than all of the other Christmas babies, and his story was special.

Rebecca started crying again and Rachel jumped up and walked over to Dorcas and little Caleb. She tentatively reached out and touched Dorcas' arm. "I'm sorry, Mrs. Stolzfus. I love Caleb and you a-n-d *ve* only *vanted* to save him."

Dorcas studied Rachel's face for a full minute. Then she gave the child a big smile.

"*Vould* you like to hold Caleb again?"

"*Ja*, yes, please!" and the child's smile lit up her entire face.

Anna McLean's Herbal Recipe for Anxiety*

(Simplified)

1 tablespoon	Chamomile tincture
½ teaspoon	Ginger Root tincture
1 teaspoon	Lavender tincture
2 teaspoons	Lemon Balm tincture
½ teaspoon	Valerian Root tincture

Place all ingredients in a small, dark-colored glass jar and shake vigorously. Store in a cool, dark place for one week and shake contents 2-3 times a day to allow the individual ingredients to blend together.

Use ¼ - ½ teaspoon every four hours as needed for anxiety and stress.

*Please note, this is for informational purposes only and is not intended for medicinal use.

About Crystal Linn

Crystal Linn is a multi-published author and co-author of the top-selling <u>Amish Forever</u> series, along with Roger Rheinheimer. She is an award-winning poet.

When Ms. Linn is not writing or teaching about writing she enjoys reading mysteries, writing poetry and sailing with friends and family. She lives in Washington State with her family and their small dog, Alex.

Contact information:

> information@crystallinn.com
>
> https://www.facebook.com/crystal.linn.
>
> www.crystallinn.com
>
> www.martinsmuses.com

Other books by Ms. Linn:

> <u>Amish Forever</u>: Co-authored with Roger Rheinheimer, the top-selling Amish Forever stories are a series of twelve volumes, telling the adventures of Ava Troyer, a young Amish woman, and her three older brothers, all living with their Aunt Rachael in Lancaster County, Pennsylvania.
>
> > E-books available on Amazon
>
> <u>Amish Forever – The Complete Series</u>: This book combines all twelve volumes in one book.
>
> > E-books available on Amazon
> >
> > Print books available on Amazon and Barnes & Noble

<u>Amish Forever – A New Journey</u>: Co-authored with Roger Rheinheimer, this top-selling series contains ten volumes which continue the adventures of the now-married Ava, along with those of her brothers and friends.

E-books available on Amazon

<u>From the Heart:</u> A small anthology of inspirational writings on nurturing the inner child.

E-books available on Amazon

Print books available directly from Ms. Linn

<u>New Beginnings, A Collection of Christmas Stories</u>: This book contains three short Christmas stories by Ms. Linn and an Amish Christmas novella written by Ms. Buroker.

E-books available on Amazon

Print books available on Amazon

<u>Yesterday, Today and Tomorrow, An Anthology</u>: Ms. Linn was the editor and a contributing author to this anthology.

Books available on Amazon

www.ingramcontent.com/pod-product-compliance
Lightning Source LLC
Chambersburg PA
CBHW060631130626
46555CB00002B/748